The WISH LIBRARY
The Wish That Got Away

The WISH LIBRARY

The Wish That Got Away

Christine Evans

illustrated by Patrick Corrigan

ALBERT WHITMAN & COMPANY
CHICAGO, ILLINOIS

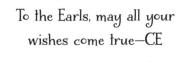

To the Earls, may all your
wishes come true—CE

To Edie and George—PC

Library of Congress Cataloging-in-Publication
data is on file with the publisher.

Text copyright © 2022 by Christine Evans
Illustrations copyright © 2022 by Albert Whitman & Company
Illustrations by Patrick Corrigan
First published in the United States of America in 2022
by Albert Whitman & Company
ISBN 978-0-8075-8747-8 (hardcover)
ISBN 978-0-8075-8748-5 (ebook)

Printed in the United States of America
10 9 8 7 6 5 4 3 2 1 LB 26 25 24 23 22 21

Design by Aphelandra

For more information about Albert Whitman & Company,
visit our website at www.albertwhitman.com.

Contents

CHAPTER 1

A New Method

"Ugh. School tomorrow!" Luca Flores groaned as he kicked a soccer ball across the yard. Luca loved weekends. There was soccer, dance, cookie baking, frozen yogurt eating. And, most importantly, no school. *I wish the weekend would never end*, Luca thought to himself.

"I can't wait!" Raven Rose called back, stopping the ball with her foot. "Ms. Earl said she'd tell us about the fall STEAM fair."

Raven loved weekends too, but she also loved

science, history, and writing about science and history. And that's what the STEAM fair was all about. She didn't even mind class presentations these days, after all that had happened with the Wish Library.

The Wish Library was a secret, magical place where any wish Raven or Luca dreamed up could come true. The only problem was, the wishes didn't always go as planned. Raven and Luca's first

wishes had caused more trouble than they were worth. On the bright side, fixing magical problems had made things like talking in front of the class seem easy-peasy.

"So I was just thinking," said Luca. "Now that we know lots of the things that can go wrong at the Wish Library, maybe we could try a new wish. One that won't go wrong."

A whole summer had passed without Raven and

Luca visiting the magical library. Partly because it was on school grounds and partly because they wanted to pick their next wish carefully.

"I don't know." Raven kicked the ball back. "I'm still worried we won't get the wish quite right."

"Well, you're the scientist," said Luca. "How about we take a scientific approach? We shouldn't waste the chance to have amazing wishes just because of a few mistakes."

The friends walked up to Luca's porch, where Mrs. Flores had left a plate of cookies for them to share with their little sisters. Izzy and Phoebe were playing jump rope in the driveway.

"What are you doing?" shouted Phoebe.

"Talking," Luca called back to his sister.

"We want to talk too!" shouted Izzy. The girls stopped jumping and ran to the porch. All four kids grabbed cookies and flopped onto the steps.

"What are we talking about?" asked Izzy.

"Me and Raven are thinking about how to make a new wish," Luca said. "Safely."

Izzy and Phoebe squirmed. They had learned about the Wish Library at the end of the last school year. Their first wish hadn't gone so well either.

"Let's make a chart," Raven suggested. "We'll list the wishes we've made so far and how they went wrong." Raven looked through her backpack

and found her notebook and pen. She made a chart with two columns:

Wish	Result
Raven: I wish for school to be canceled	A giant snowstorm came to town
Luca: I wish to be in charge	Luca actually became Principal Dawkins
Phoebe and Izzy: We wish Raven and Luca did everything together again	Raven and Luca literally got stuck together

When she was done, Raven looked at each wish. "The first wish went wrong because I wasn't exact with my wish," she said. "I just wanted school to be canceled on Voices of History Day. I *didn't* want a giant snowstorm to shut everything down."

"Yeah. My wish was pretty fun until I lost the test tube that held the wish," said Luca.

"And our wish went wrong because we *broke* the test tube!" said Izzy.

Raven wrote down the problems they'd had and then added another header after the chart:

Conclusions
Do NOT lose or drop the test tube
Word wishes carefully
Work together to plan the wish

"So what should we wish for?" asked Luca.

"Let's start small," said Raven.

"Okay," said Luca. "I wish the weekend lasted forever."

"That is not small," said Raven. "And we can't say 'forever.' Remember, every wish has to be returned."

"Fine," said Luca. "I wish for no homework then."

"Hey, I like homework!" said Raven. "We get math homework tomorrow."

"Exactly," said Luca. "Missing math homework would make Mondays way better."

Raven tapped her pen on her notebook. "All right," she said finally. "But I only want to miss *one* day's homework." She started writing on a fresh page.

Wish	Result
I wish for Ms. Earl to give us no math homework on Monday	

"We can fill in the result before school on Tuesday," said Raven. "Then we can analyze the data. Just like a science experiment."

"What about us?" asked Phoebe.

"You can choose the next wish," Raven promised. "As long as there aren't any surprises, that is."

CHAPTER 2

Success?

The next day, Luca, Raven, Phoebe, and Izzy went to school early to make their wish. When they reached the Wish Library, everything was just as they remembered. The wish computer whirred, the stern Librarian gave them her warnings, Sebastian the bearded dragon retrieved their wish, and they left with a test tube filled with glittering liquid.

Then in the forest by the wishing well, Raven followed the wish's instructions. She dropped three drops from the test tube onto her backpack and three onto Luca's. When she was done, a firework erupted over their heads.

"It seems like the wish is working," Luca said as they walked toward school. "Now we just need to see what happens."

"Good luck!" said Izzy. She and Phoebe jogged to their first-grade classroom.

Raven and Luca turned down the hallway that led to Ms. Earl's room. Ms. Earl had been their teacher last year too. They were excited she'd moved up to third grade with them.

"Gooood morning, class!" Ms. Earl sang as they filed into the room. "I'll take attendance, then I have an announcement to make."

Raven could hardly sit still. She was brimming with ideas for the STEAM fair, and unlike Luca, she was looking forward to getting started.

"As you know," Ms. Earl continued, "every fall, Lincoln Elementary hosts a STEAM fair. Now that you're in third grade, you get to present your own projects!" Ms. Earl clapped in excitement. "Let's get into teams of two or three and start discussing ideas."

The room erupted in chatter as kids got into groups. Raven and Luca teamed up, as always. Grace and Felicity. Milo, Owen, and Evie. Sam and Kira. And before long, the whole class was busy talking about the STEAM fair.

"What should we do?" Raven asked, pulling out her notebook. "I have a few ideas..."

"The science of wishes!" said Luca. "We've already started that experiment."

Raven shook her head. "That's our *secret* experiment. We can't tell anyone about it." After all the strange things that had happened around Lincoln Elementary in the past year, the last thing Raven wanted was to get more kids interested in wishes.

Luca groaned. "So we have to do two experiments?"

"We *get* to," said Raven, suddenly feeling better about wishing away her math homework.

After a few minutes, there was a knock at the door. The school admin, Ms. Bennett, peered into the classroom. "Excuse me, Ms. Earl. I have a newcomer for you," she said. Behind her was a girl in a unicorn shirt and pink leggings. "This is Lily Davis. She just moved here from England."

"Of course, Lily, welcome! I'm so happy to

meet you," said Ms. Earl. "I'm Ms. Earl, and these
are your classmates. We're just talking about our
upcoming STEAM fair projects. How about you
take a seat with Raven and Luca?"

Raven waved the new girl over. "Hi, Lily. I'm Raven," she said.

"And I'm Luca," said Luca. "I was new last year," he added.

"Hello," said Lily quietly. She sat down.

"Do you like STEAM?" asked Raven.

"I guess?" said Lily.

"We're trying to think of a project," said Luca. "Any ideas?"

"Umm," said Lily. "I don't know."

"Give her a chance," said Raven. "She just got here."

But before they could talk about their ideas, Ms. Earl clapped her hands. "You will have more time to discuss your projects this week," she said. "Let's move on to cursive practice. Then it'll be time for recess."

When the bell rang, Luca and Raven ran to the playground.

Luca stopped. He remembered recess when he had first moved to Lincoln. He'd felt lonely, like no one was on his side. It wasn't until he became best friends with Raven that things got better. "Let's ask Lily to join us," he said.

Raven and Luca searched the playground but couldn't find Lily.

After a few minutes, they spotted her at the edge of the forest where the entrance to the Wish Library was hidden. Raven wondered if they should join her, but Lily looked like she wanted to be alone.

"We can invite her to hang out during lunch," said Raven.

But during lunch, they couldn't find Lily in the cafeteria or on the playground. And through art and math, they hardly had any chance to talk with her. Then, at the end of the day, the big announcement came.

"Good news!" Ms. Earl said after the lesson. "No math homework!"

The whole class cheered. Raven and Luca high-fived. Their wish had worked! And it hadn't taken a snowstorm—or worse—to make it happen.

After school Raven and Luca fetched their bikes and waited for Izzy and Phoebe to join them. As they were waiting, Raven noticed something strange.

She pointed through the fence toward the forest. "Is that a...horse?" she asked.

"What? Where?" Luca peered through the fence. He saw something white flash between the trees. "Weird! Maybe someone is using the forest for a riding lesson?"

"Maybe..." said Raven. Luca was probably right. There was a stable nearby, after all. Still Raven knew that if something strange was happening in the forest, there was a good chance a wish was involved. But if it wasn't their wish, whose was it?

CHAPTER 3

Something Magical

The next morning before school, Raven, Luca, Izzy, and Phoebe met on Raven and Izzy's porch. Almost a full day had passed. It was time to review their wish.

"It seems like everything worked as planned," said Luca. "We got what we asked for, and nothing went wrong."

"Right," said Raven. She took out her notebook to fill in the result of their wish experiment. "At least nothing we know about." She hadn't forgotten about the strange white horse they'd seen after school.

"Yay!" Phoebe clapped. "Now it's our turn!"

But before Phoebe and Izzy could come up with the next wish, the Roses' front door opened. "You four better get going," said Mrs. Rose, making a shooing motion with her hands. "You'll be late for school!"

Luca and Raven shared a panicked look. They had been so busy thinking about their wish they'd lost track of time. Being late for school would be bad, but if they were late returning a wish—even a simple one—the consequences, which were listed at the bottom of the wish contract, could be terrible. They leaped onto their bikes and waved back at Phoebe and Izzy on their scooters. "We need to get this wish back on time," Luca called. "See you later!"

Luca and Raven pedaled hard, racing down the hill to school. When they got to the chestnut tree by the edge of the forest, Luca checked his watch. "Phew!" he said. "We have ten minutes until the bell rings. I thought we were way later."

"Yeah, my mom is obsessed with timekeeping because of her job," said Raven. Mrs. Rose worked as a pilot, flying all over the world. "She hates being late, so she always makes me early."

Raven and Luca were about to go into the forest when something caught Luca's eye. Someone was on the running track that circled the school field.

"Who's that?" Luca asked. "They're speedy!"

Raven adjusted her glasses. Before she could make out who the kid was, they sped up. The kid was whizzing around so fast Raven and Luca couldn't see who it was.

"They're too speedy!" said Raven. "Do you think they found the Wish Library?"

"Let's ask the Librarian," said Luca.

Raven and Luca headed into the forest. As usual they recited the spell to return their wish. And as usual they tumbled down the wishing well into the Wish Library. But when they landed on the trampoline at the bottom, they could tell something very *unu*sual had happened. A siren blared. A light on top of the wish computer flashed fire truck red. Luca covered his ears.

"What's going on?" Raven shouted over the noise.

"Where's the Librarian?" Luca shouted back.

"I'm right here. No need to shout," said the Librarian. Her hair was sticking out in all directions. Her glasses dangled from one ear. And Sebastian, who usually perched on her shoulder, was nowhere to be seen. She clattered some keys on the computer, and the alarm stopped.

"What's going on?" Raven repeated.

"Something very serious," the Librarian replied. "Nothing like this has ever happened. Well, not since the last Librarian, anyway."

"The last Librarian?" asked Raven. As far as she knew, the Librarian had always looked over the Wish Library.

"That's not important right now," the Librarian said. "What is important is this." She held out a broken vial in a cloth.

"A broken test tube?" said Luca.

"Does that mean a wish went off in the library?" Raven asked.

The Librarian nodded. "However, that isn't the worst part," she said. "Cleaning up broken wishes in the Wish Library is part of my job. I'm afraid this wish has escaped. And it's something terrible!"

Raven thought of the wishes she had seen in the library. "What is it? A fire-breathing dragon?"

"A giant ogre?" asked Luca.

"Even worse," said the Librarian. "A unicorn!"

Luca and Raven shared a look. They hadn't seen a horse after school yesterday. They had seen the wish that got away.

CHAPTER 4

Wish List

"Wow!" said Raven. "A real unicorn?"

"It is not 'wow,'" said the Librarian. "It is disastrous news."

"It doesn't sound so bad," said Luca. From all his sister had told him about unicorns, there was nothing dangerous about them. "Aren't unicorns friendly?"

"Friendly, yes," said the Librarian. "But they have great power. You see, unicorns can grant wishes. And unlike those from the Wish Library, these wishes don't need to be returned." She adjusted her glasses back into place and gave them a serious look. "I don't need to tell you how dangerous this could be. It could mean chaos, not just in Lincoln but in the whole world."

Raven and Luca nodded. "How can we help?" Raven asked.

"I need you to track it down," said the Librarian. "Wish Librarians aren't allowed to leave their libraries unattended."

"How will we find it?" Luca asked. *Although there probably aren't many places for a unicorn to hide,* he thought.

"You need to look for unusual things occurring," said the Librarian.

"There was a kid running superfast on the track earlier," said Raven. "It looked magical."

"That is precisely why the siren was blaring," said the Librarian. "Every time the unicorn grants a wish, it goes off."

"How many times has it sounded?" Luca asked.

"Four times so far," said the Librarian, fixing her hair. "I can pull up a list on the computer of every wish that's been granted."

"Can you print it for us?" asked Raven. "Maybe it will help us track down the unicorn."

The wish computer whirred until a slip of paper was printed. Raven pulled it from the printer and read it aloud.

UNICORN WISHES

1. Superstrength
2. Pancakes for every meal
3. Never-ending ice cream
4. Superspeed

"Can the computer tell us who made the wishes?" asked Raven.

"I'm afraid not," said the Librarian. "And they might have all been made by different children. Unicorns only grant wishes to children. Grown-ups can't see unicorns."

Raven had lots more questions she wanted to ask, but Luca elbowed her and pointed to the clock on the wall. They were going to be late.

Raven and Luca grabbed their backpacks, said goodbye to the Librarian, and headed to school, unsure of what they would find.

———

At recess later that morning, Luca and Raven hung upside down on the monkey bars. It was their favorite spot on the playground and a great spot to think. Nothing strange had happened during class, but they needed to come up with a plan.

"We could ask kids if they've seen the unicorn," said Luca.

"Shhhh!" said Raven. "If everyone knows about it, there'll be chaos."

"What are you talking about?" Phoebe asked as she and Izzy came over. Raven nodded at Luca.

"Have you two noticed anything…um, odd lately?" Luca asked.

"I have!" said Phoebe. "This morning one boy in our class picked his nose. I'm sure I saw him eat it."

Luca shook his head. "That's not what I mean," he said.

"Oh," said Phoebe. Her eyes grew, and she lowered her voice. "Do you mean magic?"

Raven nodded. "Any classmates doing anything unusual?"

"You mean like that?" asked Izzy. She pointed at a first grader sitting at the snack table. In front of him was a towering pile of pancakes. The other first graders stared at him as they ate their granola bars and apples.

"Yeah, like that!" said Raven. She and Luca jumped down from the monkey bars. "We need to talk to him. What's his name?"

"Aiden," said Izzy. "What's going on?"

"There's been an..." Raven paused. "Incident."

"Did Aiden find the Wish Library?" asked Phoebe.

"No..." said Luca. "So here's the thing: there's a unicorn on the loose."

"WOW!" said Phoebe and Izzy together.

"It is not 'wow,'" said Raven, mimicking the Librarian. "It is disastrous news."

She told the girls what the Librarian had said. When she was finished, she said, "Now we need to find the unicorn."

"Fast," added Luca.

Luca, Raven, Izzy, and Phoebe walked over to the snack table where Aiden was eating pancakes. As he poured on maple syrup, the four kids sat down across from him.

"Hi, Aiden," said Raven. "That's a lot of pancakes."

"Yeah, hi, Aiden," said Luca. "Where did you get them from?"

"I'm not going to tell you," said Aiden. "I promised I'd keep it secret."

"Aiden," said Izzy. "We won't tell anyone."

"Yeah, go on, Aiden," said Phoebe. "We want to know where the uni—"

"Shhh!" said Luca and Raven together. They looked around to make sure no one else had heard.

Aiden's eyes went as round as the pancakes on his plate. "You know about it?" he said.

"Yes. Where is it?" said Luca. His stomach rumbled. Part of him wanted to see what magical pancakes tasted like.

"I promised…" started Aiden.

"We know." Raven interrupted. "But this is serious. People could get hurt."

"Well, I am getting bored of pancakes now. It was fun at the start…" Aiden put his hand on his stomach. "Some new girl in third grade is hiding it in the forest."

Luca and Raven shared a look. They knew who Aiden was talking about.

"How did you find it?" asked Luca.

"I saw hoof tracks on the field after school yesterday and followed them," Aiden said.

"Thanks, Aiden!" said Luca.

The bell rang for the end of recess, and Raven and Luca headed back to class. "We'll find the tracks at lunch," said Raven. "Right now we need to talk to Lily."

CHAPTER 5

Following the Clues

Back in class there was no sign of Lily. But Ms. Earl didn't say anything about her absence, which was weird.

Luca and Raven hardly listened as their teacher read aloud from the book the class was reading together. *Had Lily made another wish to get out of class?* Raven wondered.

"Luca, Raven," said Ms. Earl. She had stopped reading and was looking right at them. "Are you with us?"

"Yes, sorry!" said Raven, nudging Luca.

The two friends pretended to listen until the bell rang for lunch. As soon as it sounded, they ran outside to the school field.

"Can you see any tracks?" asked Luca.

"Nothing!" said Raven. "Maybe the kids playing soccer at recess trampled over them and made them disappear."

"What are we going to do?" asked Luca.

"Let's look for more clues," said Raven. "Have you got the list the Librarian gave us?"

Luca pulled the list from his pocket. "We found the kid with pancakes for every meal," he said. "Let's head to the cafeteria to see if we can find anyone else who made a wish."

In the cafeteria, Raven and Luca spotted their sisters eating hot lunches. It was always pizza on Tuesdays. Luca's stomach gurgled. "Can we get pizza before we look for the other wishes?" he asked.

Raven led the way to the lunch counter. She was hungry too, and she needed fuel to hunt for a missing unicorn.

As the two of them sat down, Raven spotted something. Evie from Ms. Earl's class was bent over a bowl of ice cream. There was no ice cream on the menu. Raven stood up and moved along the table to sit by Evie.

"Hi," Raven said. "Where'd you get that ice cream?"

"Nowhere!" Evie said. "I didn't get it nowhere."

"Evie," said Luca, who had also moved seats. "We know about the..." Luca lowered his voice to a whisper. "Unicorn."

"We just want to know where it is," said Raven. "So, um, we can make a wish too!" She couldn't tell Evie the real reason they needed to find the unicorn. No one knew about the Wish Library, and it was forbidden to tell anyone about it.

"Okay then. I found it in the school garden

munching on kale," she said. "That new girl said I could make a wish on it. So I wished for never-ending ice cream."

As she scooped out the last of the ice cream from the bowl, a fresh bowl appeared. "Mmm, strawberry!"

"Thanks, Evie!" said Luca. Luca and Raven dashed out of the cafeteria, stacking their trays on their way out the door.

"Walk, please!" called a lunch supervisor as they ran. They slowed to a power walk until they were out of sight. Then they sprinted to the school garden.

In the garden it was clear a large animal had been stomping around. The kale had been chomped. The flowers were destroyed. But there was no sign the unicorn was still around.

"How are we going to find them?" asked Raven. "Lily and the unicorn couldn't have just vanished!"

"We could head back to the Wish Library," suggested Luca. "Maybe we can make a wish to find the unicorn?"

"Good idea!" said Raven.

⌒

In the Wish Library, the alarm was sounding again. The Librarian was holding a candlestick-shaped device that had a dial and numbers on it. She was talking into a receiver on the end of a cord.

"Yes, I understand, sir," she said. "I'm working

on containing the situation as we speak."

"Is it some kind of ancient phone?" Luca asked quietly.

Raven shrugged.

The Librarian slammed the device down and turned off the wish computer alarm.

"That was headquarters!" said the Librarian. "They're threatening to send down some investigators. I might lose my job!" The Librarian clasped her hands together. Her voice shook as she spoke. Raven and Luca had never seen her so worried.

"Headquarters?" asked Raven. "Is there more than one Wish Library?"

"We have branches all over the world," said the

Librarian. "But this is the first time a unicorn has become lost. Other creatures have escaped from time to time, but none that can grant wishes."

"How many more wishes have been granted?" asked Luca.

The Librarian clattered keys on the wish computer. "Here's the list of the latest wishes," she said, passing a printout to Luca. "At this rate the whole school will be overrun with wishes!"

ᎶNICORN WISHES continued

5. Ms. Earl to not notice I'm absent
6. Know all the answers
7. Pets!

Luca pointed at number five on the list. "That must be from Lily. Now we know why Ms. Earl didn't mention her missing class."

"Can we borrow a wish to return the unicorn?" asked Raven.

"No, HQ has suspended all borrowing until the

unicorn has been captured," said the Librarian. "The only way to fix this mess is to get the creature back to the Library."

Raven and Luca gulped. They had fixed problems with wishes before. But fixing a whole list of wishes was something completely different. Could they save the Librarian's job—and their school—before it was too late?

CHAPTER 6

Pet Problems

"Hurry, the bell will ring soon," Raven said as she and Luca jogged across the field after leaving the library. "We need to find the other wishes."

The Librarian had been talking to someone at HQ again when they left, reassuring them it was all under control. Raven wasn't so sure it was. Maybe HQ *should* send someone to help them. What could two kids do to stop a magical unicorn? Raven reminded herself she'd stopped a magical snowstorm from destroying Lincoln. She could do this.

"Who's that over there?" Luca said. He pointed at someone sitting behind the sports-equipment shed. "Maybe they've seen the unicorn."

"Good idea," said Raven. "Let's go ask."

"It's Milo from our class," said Luca as they got closer. They heard a strange squeaking noise. "What's he holding?"

"Hey, Milo," said Raven. At the sound of her voice, Milo looked up and hid something behind his back. "What are you hiding?"

"Nothing!" said Milo.

Squeak! A guinea pig jumped to the ground behind Milo and scurried away.

Raven scooped it up. "Cute!" she said. "What's her name?"

"Primrose," said Milo. "Don't let anyone see her!"

"Why do you have a pet at school?" asked Luca. Before Milo could answer, Luca had an idea. He took the list from his pocket and looked at Wish #7: *Pets!* He looked at Raven.

"Did you see Lily?" asked Raven. "And her... friend?"

Milo nodded. A goldfish in a bowl suddenly appeared beside him.

"Woah!" said Luca. "I've always wanted a pet fish."

"Me too," said Milo. "But pets keep appearing. I can't hide them all, and my mom will never let me keep them."

"What else has appeared?" asked Raven.

"A rabbit. She's munching vegetables in the garden," said Milo. "And a parrot who's flying around the forest. I'm going to get them after school."

"My dad can help look after them," said Raven. "He's a zookeeper. Bring them to my house after school."

Milo looked relieved. He nodded.

The bell rang, and Luca, Raven, and Milo (with the guinea pig in one hand and the goldfish bowl in the other) walked to class. As they walked, a chicken appeared behind them.

"Milo, it is *not* Bring Your Pet to School Day," said Ms. Earl. "Please take them to the office." Milo sighed and left the classroom. Raven hoped her dad would help him later.

"Class," Ms. Earl continued, "I want to see how much you remember from our last unit about the geography of California."

Luca groaned. He couldn't even remember the name of the state capital.

"What is the name of the mountain range to the east?" asked Ms. Earl.

"Sierra Nevada!" shouted Felicity.

"Very good, Felicity, but let's raise our hand next time," said Ms. Earl. "And what is the name of the ocean to the west?"

"Pacific!" Felicity shouted again.

"Felicity! Please refrain from shouting." Ms. Earl looked slightly annoyed. "Someone else this time, please. Can someone name a desert?"

"Mojave!" said Felicity. Her face had turned bright red.

"Felicity! Please sit outside if you can't stop shouting answers," Ms. Earl said with her hands on her hips. Felicity ran from the room with her hands over her mouth.

That was strange, Raven thought. Felicity almost never answered questions in class unless she was called on. Then Raven remembered the Librarian's wish list: *Know all the answers.*

"Ms. Earl!" Raven called. "Should I check on her?"

"Yes, please, Raven," said Ms. Earl. "Class, what is the capital of California?"

Luca exchanged looks with Raven as she stood up to leave the classroom.

"Sacramento," she whispered in his ear before joining Felicity outside.

Raven found Felicity on the bench in the hallway. "Are you okay?" she asked.

"I couldn't help it," said Felicity. Her head was in her hands, and tears rolled down her face.

Raven put her arm around her friend. "I know," she said. "I can help if you can tell me where Lily is hiding the unicorn."

Felicity looked up at Raven. "You know about the unicorn?"

"Yeah. And it's dangerous," said Raven. "We need to stop it."

"I thought it would be fun to know all the answers, but it's terrible!" said Felicity. "I hate being in trouble with Ms. Earl."

"Can you show us after school where you made your wish?" asked Raven.

"Yes," said Felicity. "Grace can help too. She made a wish for superspeed, but her legs are hurting too much to keep running."

"It isn't just you two," said Raven. "Everybody's wishes are starting to go wrong. Well, except for Evie. She seemed pretty happy at lunchtime with—"

The door to the classroom swung open. It was Evie, clutching her stomach.

"Too much ice cream!" she moaned. "I'm going to the nurse's office."

"I'll see you after school," Raven told Felicity. She opened the door to go back to class. *I just hope the school won't be overrun with wishes by then,* she thought. A snake slithered through the doorway. *Or pets.*

CHAPTER 7

Raven's Plan

After school Felicity, Grace, Luca, Raven, Izzy, and Phoebe met at the edge of the forest.

"We don't have long. Our parents will wonder where we are," said Raven. "Let's split up. Me, Grace, and Izzy in one group. Luca, Felicity, and Phoebe in the other. Meet back here in fifteen minutes."

Raven led her group into the forest. "Grace, where did you meet Lily and the unicorn?" she asked.

"It was in a clearing," said Grace. "This way." In a blink, Grace raced off with her superspeed.

"Slow down!" Raven called.

"Sorry," Grace said, racing back. "I can't help it!" Grace ran back and forth along the path until she led them all to the spot where she'd last seen Lily.

In the clearing, they found glittery poop and a trail of hoofprints.

"Let's follow the trail," said Raven.

Meanwhile, Luca and Phoebe followed Felicity in the opposite direction.

"I saw them by the fence," Felicity said. She stopped by the fence that separated the edge of the forest from the rest of the town. The bars of the fence had been pulled apart by someone superstrong. The gap was big enough to fit a unicorn through.

"They've escaped!" said Luca. "How are we going to find them now? Let's tell Raven."

"I'm right here!" said Raven, jogging up behind Luca. "We followed a trail from the clearing."

"Do you have a plan?" asked Izzy, looking up at her big sister. Raven started to shake her head. But then she got an idea. "Actually, I do. Follow me!"

Milo was waiting on Raven's porch when she arrived. He had the goldfish and its bowl, Primrose the guinea pig, a rabbit, a chicken, and a parrot sitting on his shoulder.

"I couldn't find the snake," said Milo. "I hope it's okay."

"You'd better wait here while I get my dad," said Raven. "You all head inside," Raven added to Felicity, Grace, Luca, Phoebe, and Izzy.

Mr. Rose came to the door. "Well, young Milo, that's quite the menagerie you have there. Come out back. I have somewhere safe for the rabbit, chicken, parrot, and guinea pig to hang out while we find them somewhere new to live. And I've always wanted a goldfish."

"I told him you'd rescued them," whispered Raven. "I couldn't tell him about the you-know-what!"

Milo followed Mr. Rose, and Raven headed inside. She collected paper, crayons, and pens. Phoebe, Izzy, Felicity, Grace, and Luca were waiting at the kitchen table.

"We're going to make posters," Raven said. "Hopefully someone will have seen the missing 'horse.'"

Over the next hour, the six of them made dozens of posters.

"You all put these posters up around town," Raven said. "I'll put the other part of my plan into action."

Grace took the stack of posters. "I can get these on all the lampposts in town in a few minutes!" she said. Before Raven could reply, she'd whizzed out of the house.

"Okay. In that case, everyone, meet me in the backyard. I'll be there soon!" Raven said. Before she left the house, she picked up a box from the playroom. "Izzy, can you bring this outside with you?" she asked.

Raven hoped her plan would work.

CHAPTER 8

My Only Friend

Raven jumped onto her bike and cycled from house to house, asking classmates if they wanted to come out to play. The group of kids followed Raven to her backyard. She climbed up on top of an old plastic slide her parents had never thrown out.

"Attention, everyone!" she said. Everyone quieted down and stared back at her. She took a deep breath. *I can do hard things!* she thought. "A horse has escaped, and I need everyone's help to find it."

The crowd whispered. Some of the kids knew it

wasn't really a horse, but Raven hoped they'd keep it a secret. If the others knew it was a unicorn, they might try to find it and make even more wishes.

"I'll help!" said Evie, who was feeling better after eating her ice cream.

Sam, Owen, and Kira all agreed too.

"Has anyone seen or heard anything strange?" asked Raven.

"I heard a horse neighing outside my house after school," said Sam. "But when I looked, there was nothing there."

Raven took out a map of the neighborhood. She marked the school field, the garden, and Sam's house.

"I found hoofprints in my backyard," said Evie. She showed Raven her house on the map.

Milo raised his hand. He now had a Labrador on a leash. "My dog could help us track the..." He paused. "*Horse*'s scent." Milo winked at Raven.

"Great idea! Milo and I will follow the dog," said Raven. "We'll start at Sam's house to get the scent. Everyone else, check the backyards in the neighborhood. Luca, call me if anyone finds anything," She took a walkie-talkie out of Izzy's box, and handed it to Luca. She put another one in her pocket and waved to Milo. "Let's go!"

At Sam's house the Labrador pulled on the leash. "She can smell something!" said Milo. Milo and Raven followed the dog through the streets of Lincoln.

"What's that noise?" Raven said after a little while. She held up her hand for Milo to stop. The noise sounded like... "Horse hooves!" she said.

Milo's dog strained at the leash and pulled them on.

"There they are!" said Raven. She saw the backside of the unicorn disappear around the next corner.

Raven, Milo, and the dog followed the scent until they reached the school fence with the unicorn-sized hole. "They must have gone back into the forest to hide," said Raven.

Raven took the walkie-talkie from her pocket. "Come in, Luca. This is Raven. Meet me in the forest. Over."

"Thanks, Milo," said Raven. "Can you two go back and tell the others they can stop searching?"

Milo waved and ran back toward the neighborhood with his dog. A goat was now following him. Raven noticed an owl flying overhead too.

Luca came running to the school. He did a double take at the animals now following Milo up the hill. Raven waited while Luca got his breath back. "Was that an owl?" he asked.

Raven nodded with a laugh. Then she turned toward the hole in the fence. "We need to find Lily," she said. "What if the next 'pet' that appears is an elephant? Or something even worse!"

"Good point," said Luca. "Let's go."

Luca and Raven clambered through the fence and followed the hoofprints.

"I can hear someone," whispered Raven. "It must be Lily."

Raven and Luca crept through the trees. Luca stepped on a stick, and it snapped with a crack.

"Shhhh!" said Raven.

"Who's there?" said a voice. Raven and Luca walked into the clearing. Lily was standing next to a beautiful white unicorn. Its mane and tail were rainbow-colored, and its horn was glowing gold.

Lily stroked the unicorn's mane. "Don't come any nearer," she said. "Why have you been chasing us?"

"We need to send the unicorn home," said Raven. "She's dangerous."

"No! She's my only friend in this whole town,"

said Lily. "In fact she's my only friend in the whole country."

Lily whispered something into the unicorn's ear. A plume of rainbow smoke engulfed Lily and the unicorn. Raven and Luca coughed and waved the smoke away.

"Where'd they go?" said Luca.

"I think she made a wish to disappear!" said Raven. The friends looked around the forest. There was no sign of Lily or the unicorn.

CHAPTER 9
All the Answers

"Now what?" Raven asked. They had tried everything.

Luca shook his head. "I don't know. But I do know how Lily feels. It can be hard to make new friends in a new place." When he was new at Lincoln Elementary, he hadn't known anyone. Even after he and Raven had become friends, there were still times he'd felt like the lonely new kid.

"We need to show her she can make friends here," said Raven. "And that we want to be her friends."

"How are we going to do that if she keeps running away?" said Luca.

"Have you still got the lists of wishes?" asked Raven. "Maybe there's a clue there to how we can find her."

Luca dug in his pockets. As well as the lists from the Librarian, he found two quarters and a stick of bubble gum. He popped the gum into his mouth.

"Chewing helps me think," he said. He read through the wishes. "Superstrength, pancakes, ice cream, superspeed, all the answers, pets—"

"Yes!" said Raven.

"What?" said Luca. He blew a pink bubble. It popped in his face.

"All the answers!" said Raven. "Felicity wished to know all the answers. The wish didn't say it was answers just to school questions."

"Oh!" said Luca. "We can ask Felicity where Lily is now!"

"One of us needs to run back to find her," said Raven.

"I have a better idea," said Luca. "I gave my walkie-talkie to Phoebe so I could let her know when we'd found Lily and the unicorn."

"Brilliant!" said Raven. She took her walkie-talkie out of her pocket and pushed the button.

"Come in, Phoebe. It's Raven. Can you hear me?" There was just a scratchy static noise. She tried again. No answer.

"Maybe we're out of range," said Luca. "Let's walk to the edge of the forest."

Raven tried again when they reached the fence. "Phoebe, it's Raven. Are you there?"

"Hello?" Phoebe said over the walkie-talkie. "Can you hear me?"

"I can hear you. Is Felicity there?" Raven asked. There was a long pause.

"I'm here," said Felicity.

"We need your help," said Raven. "We need you to answer a question."

"Okay, I'll try!" said Felicity.

"Where is Lily?" Raven asked.

"In the school garden," Felicity answered. "Woah! How did I do that?"

"You wished to know all the answers!" said Raven. "We've got to go. Thanks!"

Luca and Raven dashed through the forest. "We need to be careful," said Luca. "She might vanish again."

"Let's talk about how we want to be friends," said Raven.

As Luca and Raven approached the garden, there was no sign of Lily or the unicorn.

"Maybe Felicity got it wrong," said Luca.

"I don't think so," whispered Raven. "Look!"

She pointed to an apple tree in the corner of the garden. Apples were disappearing, one by one, as if they were being plucked by something large and invisible.

"Lily, I know what it's like," said Luca. "I know how it feels when you don't have any friends."

"And we know what it's like when you feel scared of something," Raven added. "Sometimes you want to wish the hard thing away. But that doesn't fix things. Not really."

Raven nodded at Luca to keep talking.

"We can help," said Luca. "We want to be friends."

Raven and Luca waited. *I hope this works,* thought Raven.

CHAPTER 10

I Wish No More!

Just as Raven was about to tell Luca to give up and try something else, a rainbow shot into the sky. Beneath the rainbow, the unicorn and Lily appeared.

Lily patted the unicorn, whispered something in her ear, and walked over to Raven and Luca.

"Did you mean it?" said Lily. She had tears brimming in her eyes.

"Yes!" said Raven. "We do want to be your friends. And so does our whole class."

"I thought I could get them to be my friends by granting wishes," said Lily. "But then they still didn't come back to play with me."

"Their wishes got out of control," said Luca. "Evie got a stomachache from all the ice cream. Milo has a whole zoo following him around. Felicity got in trouble for blurting out in class. And Grace's legs hurt from running all the time."

"Oh no!" said Lily. She started to cry then. "I just wanted them to be my friends."

"We know you didn't mean for anything to go wrong," said Raven. "We have some experience with wishes not going the way we planned."

"My own wishes didn't go right either," said Lily. "I broke my mum's favorite vase with my superstrength. It had been my grandma's, and we brought it all the way from England."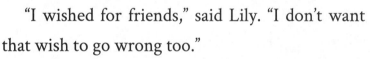

"What other wishes did you make?" asked Luca.

"I wished for friends," said Lily. "I don't want that wish to go wrong too."

"You don't need to make a wish to make friends," said Raven. "We want to be your friends anyway."

"We can help you fix the wishes that went wrong and help the unicorn get home," said Luca. "Will you come with us?"

Lily nodded and walked back to the unicorn. "I wish for you to follow me," she said.

A shower of silver sparkles burst from the unicorn's horn, and she bowed her head to Lily.

"We're going to take you to an unusual place," said Raven. "We promise everything will be fine."

At the spot in the forest where the entrance to the Wish Library was hidden, Luca and Raven realized there was a problem.

"Um, how are we going to get the unicorn down the well?" asked Luca.

Raven shook her head. She had no idea. It definitely wouldn't fit.

"A well?" asked Lily nervously. "What well?" She looked around.

"I know!" said Luca. "We should just return it the same way we return all the wishes."

"Yes!" said Raven. "Let's say it together. Repeat after us, Lily."

"I wish no more. I wish no more. I wish no more!" said Luca and Raven. Lily repeated the phrase too. The wishing well entrance appeared, and the unicorn vanished!

Luca jumped into the wishing well, followed by Raven, who shouted back to Lily, "Don't worry. Follow us!"

Luca and Raven landed on the trampoline and looked around. Things seemed calmer. There was no flashing red alarm, for one thing. The Librarian swooped into the library's main chamber just as Lily landed on the trampoline. Lily gazed around as if in a trance.

The Librarian was holding a test tube full of rainbow sparkles as well as a bigger metal tube. "You did it!" she said. "HQ sent this special secure container to make sure the unicorn doesn't escape again."

She placed the test tube inside the metal tube and screwed the lid tight. Then she entered a four-digit code on the lid.

"Is your job safe?" asked Luca.

"Oh yes, there was never any doubt," said the Librarian. "I knew all would be well."

Raven was glad the Librarian had so much confidence in them.

"This is Lily," said Raven. "What happened to all the wishes she and the other kids made?"

"When the unicorn was returned, so were all the wishes," said the Librarian. "All the pets, superpowers, food, and so on. No lasting damage. Hopefully."

"Phew!" said Luca.

"I'm going to have Sebastian put this in a safe place," said the Librarian, walking away. "Don't touch anything!"

"Where are we?" asked Lily, her mouth wide like a fish's. "Who was that? What's happening?"

"This is the Wish Library," said Raven.

"And that was the Librarian," Luca added.

"Don't worry. We'll explain everything on the way home," said Raven.

"Wait until you hear about the bearded dragon!" Luca laughed.

CHAPTER 11

Final Results

"Raven, Izzy," called Mr. Rose. "Luca and Phoebe are waiting for you."

Raven and Izzy put their water bottles and snacks into their backpacks and joined their friends at the front door. This morning they had one more stop on the way to school.

Lily was waiting for them on her front porch. She waved shyly.

"Hi, Lily!" said Raven. "I'm excited to start our STEAM project today."

"Me too," said Lily. "I brought some books to help us." She patted her backpack.

"I hope Ms. Earl likes our idea!" said Raven.

At school Ms. Earl took attendance and asked everyone to get into their project groups. They were going to spend the whole day working on them.

Lily, Raven, and Luca sat around a table and got out their supplies.

"Remember, you need to make a poster and be prepared to answer questions from people visiting your display," said Ms. Earl. "We'll visit each other's displays after lunch so you can practice answering questions."

"Let's start with the title," said Raven.

"How about, 'Is It a Unicorn?'" said Luca.

"Or 'Are Unicorns Real?'" said Lily.

"That's perfect, Lily!" said Raven.

Luca took out some markers and started the lettering.

"Now we need to find evidence to complete our

poster," said Raven. Of course, they now knew the truth. But they wanted to know if there were any other signs of unicorns throughout history.

The three kids worked together all morning making their poster. They researched narwhals and rhinoceroses. In a science magazine, they even found evidence of a one-horned deer.

"Look at this!" said Luca, pointing at another creature on the computer screen. "I can draw one of these for the poster."

"Woah!" said Lily and Raven together. Luca

grinned and started drawing. He wasn't a fan of homework, but art was his favorite subject.

—

After lunch Ms. Earl clapped her hands to get everyone's attention. "Now it's time to visit each other's displays and ask questions."

Owen, Milo, and Evie had worked together on their poster titled "How Dogs Use Their Noses to Help Humans." It had pictures of dogs doing different jobs, like working with the police and helping after disasters.

Felicity and Grace's poster was about the fastest animals on the planet. Sam and Kira had explored the different tracks animals leave behind, from hoofprints to scat. Then everyone came to Luca, Raven, and Lily's display.

"We wanted to answer the question: Are unicorns real?" said Raven.

"And we discovered the answer is yes," said Lily. She was blushing slightly, but everyone smiled

encouragingly, and she carried on. "The Siberian unicorn existed tens of thousands of years ago, and it wasn't very pretty," she added.

The class laughed. Luca's drawing was certainly nothing like the beautiful creature that had granted their wishes that week.

"The Siberian unicorn had one giant horn," said Luca. "It was a type of rhino, and it was super hairy!"

"Any questions?" asked Raven.

"How do scientists know it was real?" asked Owen.

"They've found fossils of the creature," said Luca, pointing to a photo on their poster.

"Could it grant wishes?" asked Evie.

"No!" Lily, Luca, and Raven all said together.

"Wonderful projects, everyone!" said Ms. Earl. "Your homework is to finish your posters, and we'll put them on display at the STEAM fair tomorrow afternoon. Class dismissed!"

"Homework!" groaned Luca.

"You can't avoid homework forever," said Raven.

Luca grinned. Maybe he could if he made the same wish every day.

"I know what you're thinking!" said Raven. "Remember our promise? We'd come up with

86

wishes *together*! Plus, I added loads more data to my notebook, so we can figure out how to make sure our next wish turns out just right."

"Yeah, okay," said Luca. The three friends gathered their backpacks and walked out of the classroom.

Raven smiled at Luca and Lily. "So what *should* we wish for next?"

BERGNER

(*Points to the guitar.*) Does that belong to you? (*She shoves it away contemptuously.*)

VON STROHEIM

The longer I look at you, the ghostlier you seem to me.

BERGNER

And with every one of your feelings you describe to me you take a possible feeling away from me.

VON STROHEIM

I'm not describing my feelings for you.

BERGNER

But you're *intimating* them. And every time you intimate your love for me, my feelings for you grow duller and I shrivel up. Your feelings move me, but I can't respond to them, that's all. At first I loved you, you were so serious. It struck me that usually it can be said only of a child that it is "serious." Besides (*She laughs.*), you had such beautiful eating habits. You really ate beautifully! And when I once said, "I got wet to the skin!" you said, "To *your* skin!" When I speak of it I almost love you again. (*She embraces him suddenly, but immediately steps back again even farther away.*) But I only have to mention that and I become insensitive right away. You talked all the time and I forgot you more and more. Then I was startled and you were still there . . . A complete stranger, you talked to me with shameless intimacy, as to someone at the end of a movie. Do you understand? I am taboo for you! Suddenly I was taboo for you. Two seconds! Two seconds of pain, that's what having loved you will mean to me later on. (*Pause.*) I'm not disappointed, I'm not sad, I'm only tired of you. (*She moves imperceptibly under her dress.*) I have wronged you so much.

VON STROHEIM
Wronged in what way?

BERGNER
The wrong of loving you.

(PORTEN *suddenly claps her hands vehemently,* GEORGE
laughs offensively, VON STROHEIM *and* BERGNER *slowly move
away from the spot and begin to walk around aimlessly in
different directions. Pause.*)

JANNINGS
(*Begins telling a story.*) A short time ago I saw a stewardess,
but an ugly one . . .

VON STROHEIM
(*Interrupts him.*) Let's talk about something else.

JANNINGS
(*Begins another story.*) Not long ago I saw a woman standing in the street, not a streetwalker, I must add . . .

GEORGE
(*Interrupts him.*) Something else!

JANNINGS
It is less than a week ago that I saw behind a bank counter
someone who had a rather long nose. But when I talked to
him, it turned out that despite . . .

PORTEN and BERGNER
(*Interrupt him.*) Let's change the subject.

JANNINGS
All right. No more than five minutes had passed when a
man in the park approached me. No, not a faggot . . .

(*He is interrupted by a girl who comes onstage from the right, a suitcase in her hand:* ALICE KESSLER. *She is wearing an afternoon dress and looks as if she had come to this performance by mistake.*)

ALICE
(*Puts down the suitcase, begins to speak very matter-of-factly.*) Is it you? Am I in the right place here? I heard you talking from a distance and came in. The sounds I heard were so inviting, voices and laughter, what is more beautiful than that? What are you showing to each other there, I'd like to see something too. What are you whispering about? I'd like to hear something too. (*She tosses her hat to* VON STROHEIM. *He is so disconcerted that he turns aside instead of catching it.*) How are you? (*Pause. All of them seem petrified.*) How are you?

BERGNER
(*Suddenly loosens up and moves. She practices her reply.*) Fine? Fine. Fine! We're fine. Indeed! We're fine! (*Pause. She tries to talk normally again.*) And how—and how are you?

ALICE
(*Answers quite naturally.*) I'm fine too. Though my hand is still trembling from carrying that heavy suitcase, and I'm still a little weak in the knees because I'm not used to wearing high-heeled shoes; but I can put up with all that because I'm so happy to see you. What are you doing here?

BERGNER
(*Is glad to be able to answer so simply.*) We're talking.

ALICE
And now you don't know how to go on?

BERGNER
Perhaps. (*She falters.*) Yes. Yes!

ALICE
Hello!

BERGNER
Hello!

ALICE
(*To the others*) Hello! (*They raise their heads, perplexed.
As if awakening, still half asleep, not knowing yet what they
are saying, they say one after the other: "Hello!" Then they
comprehend what they have said and become lively. The
stage light gradually turns into early-morning light again.*)
What time is it?

(GEORGE *nudges* JANNINGS *in the hip.*)

JANNINGS
(*As if back to sleep already*) Don't you have a watch? (*He
gives a start.*) "How late is it?" Of course: how late is it?
Well, how late is it now? You could have said so right away.
(*He opens his pocket watch in front of* ALICE.)

ALICE
Thanks! (*He shuts the watch again.*)

JANNINGS
(*After a pause.*) Don't mention it. (*He spreads his arms
wide as if he just found a solution and plays with the answer.*)
Don't mention it! (*To* GEORGE) Ask me what time it is.

GEORGE
(*Merrily*) What time is it? (JANNINGS *shows him the pocket
watch.*) Thanks!

JANNINGS
(*Shuts the watch.*) Don't mention it.

GEORGE
(*Merrily*) Thanks!

JANNINGS
(*Cheerfully*) But I insist: don't mention it!

(ALICE *holds out her hand to* JANNINGS. *He shakes it instantly. She also holds out her hand to* GEORGE *and he shakes it instantly. She holds out her hand to* PORTEN *and* PORTEN *shakes it gratefully.* VON STROHEIM *understands too and takes her hand.*
Now she takes off her gloves and everyone watches very inquisitively. She hands them to VON STROHEIM *and he takes them. He now picks up the hat and tosses it playfully to* GEORGE. GEORGE *catches the hat and puts it on the table.* VON STROHEIM *adds the gloves to it. Everything is working well.* BERGNER *sits down, apparently relieved.*)

ALICE
(*To* VON STROHEIM) What do you have there in your hand?

VON STROHEIM
(*Opens his fist.*) A necklace. Yes, a necklace!

ALICE
It's beautiful!

A VOICE
(*From the wings*) It's *not* beautiful.

(ELLEN KESSLER *now appears from the left, also with a suitcase, dressed exactly like* ALICE. *She tosses* VON STROHEIM *her hat, then takes off her gloves and hands them to him.*)

VON STROHEIM

(*Puts the things on the table and asks* ELLEN) So you would like to have it?

ALICE

(*Replies*) Yes.

(*He turns to* ALICE *and puts the necklace around her neck. She moves voluptuously.*

ELLEN *begins to walk around. She walks about with the same movements as* ALICE *did before. Shakes hands with everyone and says: "Hello!" They answer her—at least, the first two do—after an initial pause; then they laugh at each other as over a joke. Behind her back* GEORGE *takes a cigar out of the box and shows it to* JANNINGS; *then he takes out a second one; they laugh silently; finally* GEORGE *shows* JANNINGS *a third cigar,* JANNINGS *becomes serious and looks to the left and right, but no one else appears.*

In the meantime, ELLEN *taps* VON STROHEIM *on the shoulder to greet him. He is talking to* ALICE.)

VON STROHEIM

Why is it that I'm so sure I've seen you before whenever I look at you, although when I actually say it (*He turns to* ELLEN, *since she has tapped him on the shoulder, and continues talking to her as if it were quite normal.*), it strikes me as the usual cliché? (ELLEN *holds out her hand to him and he bends over it. She shies back, and* ALICE *says, "He bit me!" remaining motionless, while* ELLEN *performs the appropriate gestures.* VON STROHEIM *to* ALICE) In my imagination I was about to pinch myself in the arm.

ALICE

(*Motionless.*) Already forgotten.

VON STROHEIM
Already forgotten?

ALICE
You always ask. Were you alone too long?

VON STROHEIM
Why?

ELLEN
Or did you work too hard?

VON STROHEIM
Why?

ALICE
Or do you pose counterquestions only to win time for your reply? Because you're figuring out a lie? Because in the meantime you're so washed up that you can't answer any more without lying? I came in quietly and you all sat there looking washed up, but you looked at me as though *you* had been quiet until then, and *I*, by entering so suddenly, should actually be the one to look washed up.

VON STROHEIM
What are you talking about?

ELLEN
About you. I only wanted to show you how you talk.

(*She leans against his back, shoves one leg between his. He looks down at himself. She puts her arms around his neck.* ALICE *waves to him with a finger.* ELLEN *doubles the gesture by holding her hands to his face from the back and also bending a finger. He wants to take a step forward, and lean back at the same time, but remains standing there.*)

VON STROHEIM
I'll talk as I please.

(ELLEN *puts her hand over his eyes.*)

ALICE
Then say something.

VON STROHEIM
(*Opens his mouth and shuts it. He moves his hands as if he were looking for something that keeps eluding him. He stammers, but whenever his hand seems to seize something, he produces whole syllables:* "be, what, un, re"; *then he reaches for it and it escapes him again, and he goes on stammering.* ELLEN *takes her hands away from his eyes and he calms down instantly.*) I can't; it's like reaching for a piece of soap under water.

ALICE
What?

VON STROHEIM
Already forgotten. When you covered my eyes, I had it perfectly clear in front of me, but now I have forgotten it. (*He falters.*) "Already forgotten!" That was it! You said, "Already forgotten!" and I remembered something, but what? It escaped me again and again, and I had a feeling like searching for a piece of soap under water—(*He makes a perfunctory gesture, suddenly sniffs his fingers, repeats the gesture. Pause.*)

ELLEN
Perhaps you'll think of it . . .

ALICE
. . . if you watch me?

ELLEN

(*With a flattering voice, ambiguously.*) Perhaps, if you watch me, you'll also remember where you put me—(*She laughs.*) where you carried me to—(*She laughs.*) in those days, do you remember?—(*She laughs.*) and you'll also remember what you should do with me now. (*She laughs. Because* ELLEN *stands behind him, one does not see her talking, although* ALICE *moves her lips and makes the appropriate gestures.*)

(*They let him stand there and skip and dance across the stage side by side. With a fervent pleasure in their work, nearly parallel in their movements, they busy themselves with the objects and with the people: while one takes off* JANNINGS's *boots, the other is loosening* GEORGE's *shoelaces: finished at the same time, they begin to brush* PORTEN's *and* BERGNER's *hair; again they finish at the same time and skip over to the open drawer of the chest; they return with four fancy cushions and stuff them, running helter-skelter but with similar movements, behind the backs of the four people. There is hardly time to perceive these actions when they are already back at the table with four glasses and two bottles and they place them before the characters.*

But now their movements slow down and begin to contradict each other; the work of the one is revoked by the other: one takes the glasses and bottles which the other has placed there away again; one dishevels the hair the other has just brushed; then one takes away the cushions from the persons to whom the other has given them. At the same time the other removes the bottles and the glasses that the one . . . Then one ties the shoelaces the other has untied, while the other in the meantime is taking away the cushions from . . . whereupon the one dishevels the hair that . . . while the other puts JANNINGS's *boots back on.*

However, they stop at the same time and want to run offstage quickly in opposite directions; they return once more and change directions, finally run into the wings. As soon as they have disappeared, they cannot be heard running any more.

Everyone onstage is holding his breath. Suddenly, out of their state of complete immobilization, JANNINGS and GEORGE leap up and rush to the suitcases that have been left onstage. They fling them into the wings after ELLEN and ALICE, but no crashing sound can be heard. They listen. Then they stop listening. While they are returning to their places, PORTEN suddenly leaps up too and throws the remaining things, hats and gloves, into the wings after the girls, tossing the hats as if they were gloves, letting the gloves sail through the air as if they were hats. One hears them crashing like suitcases.

They all settle in their places.)

PORTEN
Goo—(*as in good*)

(*The others turn instantly to* BERGNER.)

PORTEN
I'm speaking. (*They turn awkwardly to her.* BERGNER *seems to have fallen asleep.*) Hello!

GEORGE
(*A little too late.*) Hello!

PORTEN
(*A little too late.*) How are you?

GEORGE
(*A little too late.*) Fine. (*A little too late.*) And how are you?

PORTEN
(*A little too late.*) Fine— Please hand me the paper.

(*A brief pause. Only then does* GEORGE *hand her the newspaper from the table. She holds it in her hand. Pause. Only then does she look into it.*)

GEORGE
Is there anything in it?

(*Pause.*)

PORTEN
(*As though she had answered immediately*) I'm just looking. (*Pause. She puts the paper away.*)

GEORGE
Give me the paper. (*Pause. Then she gives him the paper, but does so as if she had given it to him at once.* GEORGE *opens it, looks at it only after an interval. Pause. Then he exclaims as if he had seen the picture on first glance.*) Ice floes!

(*Pause.*)

PORTEN
(*Lively*) Really? (*Pause.*) How much do you weigh?

(*Pause.*)

GEORGE
Two hundred eighteen pounds.

(*Pause.*)

PORTEN
O God!

(*Pause.*)

JANNINGS
(*Shakes his head. He hesitates and looks at* GEORGE.) Why are you shaking your head? Do you want to contradict me?

GEORGE
I am neither shaking my head nor would I, even if I shook my head, thereby want to contradict you.

PORTEN
(*To* JANNINGS) You were shaking your head yourself.

JANNINGS
That was me?

VON STROHEIM
That was you.

JANNINGS
(*Looks to* GEORGE.) Who is speaking?

VON STROHEIM
I am.

JANNINGS
(*To* VON STROHEIM) That was you?

GEORGE
Yes.

JANNINGS
(*To* GEORGE) You're *talking?*

GEORGE
Are you dreaming?

JANNINGS

> Am I in earth, in heaven, or in hell?
> Sleeping or waking, mad or well-advised?
> Known unto these, and to myself disguised:
> Am I transformed, master, am not I?
> (*Pause. To* GEORGE) Do you have a match?

GEORGE

Yes.

(*Pause.* JANNINGS *points with his finger on the table, but the others look at his finger. At last he looks at his finger too and lets his hand drop. Pause.* VON STROHEIM *wants to pull out the red cloth.*)

JANNINGS

(*Sees it and screams*) No! (VON STROHEIM *puts it away again instantly. Pause.* PORTEN *begins to laugh, becomes quiet immediately.* GEORGE *looks at her questioningly, she only shakes her head. Pause.*) Let us pray to God.

PORTEN

(*Instantly*) My candy.

BERGNER

(*In her sleep*) There's a rat in the kitchen.

(*Pause.*)

VON STROHEIM

(*Reaches into the cigar box. He asks*) May I take one? (*They look at him, he pulls back his hand. He asks once more*) May I take a cigar? (*And already extends his hand. They look at him and he pulls back his hand. With arms pressed to his sides, he asks once more*) May I take one?

(No one looks at him and he takes a cigar. PORTEN *gives him the ashtray.)*

GEORGE
(To PORTEN*)* Thank you.

PORTEN
Why are you thanking me?

GEORGE
Because that would have been my job.

(Long pause. GEORGE *lifts up the teapot and puts it down again.)*

JANNINGS
(Upbraids him.) What do you mean by that?

GEORGE
(Pulls in his head. Pause. He takes out a piece of chocolate candy, removes the silver foil, and eats the candy. After he has consumed it, he asks PORTEN*)* Or did you want a piece of it? *(She doesn't reply. He stares into the paper.)* Just now I read the word *snowstorm,* and now I can't find it any more!

(All stare into the paper. Pause.)

VON STROHEIM
(To PORTEN*)* Do you have the number 23–32–322?

PORTEN
No, I have the number 233–23–22. *(Brief pause.)* In my neighborhood there is a shopping center with stores, restaurants, and . . .

VON STROHEIM
A movie house?

PORTEN

Why? (*Pause.*) I once attended a going-out-of-business sale . . .

GEORGE

And everyone screamed, ran around, and turned over the furniture?

PORTEN

No. They— Yes! They turned over the furniture, screamed, and ran around! (*She looks at him happily, becomes serious again instantly. Suddenly delighted, to* VON STROHEIM) 23–32–322? Yes, that *is* my number. (*Pause. She looks at* GEORGE *for a long time.*)

GEORGE

Why do you look at me like that?

PORTEN

I'm afraid I might not be able to recognize you again. (*She was serious when she began her reply but ended it as a joke. She cuddles her head against her shoulder. Pause.* GEORGE *lowers his head.*) Hey!

GEORGE

(*Shouts at her.*) What kind of a feeling do you have? (*He comes to his senses and asks her again kindly*) I wanted to ask you: what kind of feelings do you have?

PORTEN

Too many of them.

JANNINGS

In those days the grass smelled of dog piss before the thunderstorm.

PORTEN
Who's saying that?

JANNINGS
I?

PORTEN
I see. (*She continues at once.*) As a child, if I wanted to have
something, I always had to say first what it was called.

GEORGE
(*Wants to say something.*) And I . . .

VON STROHEIM
(*Irritated*) Yes, people showed me something and then
walked away with it—(*Contemplatively*) And I had to follow
and get it for myself.

GEORGE
(*Wants to say something.*) And I . . .

VON STROHEIM
Or people simply opened the drawer in which the thing was
and went away.

GEORGE
(*To* VON STROHEIM) And so that I could learn to get my
way—(VON STROHEIM *looks away.* GEORGE *turns to* JAN-
NINGS.) I was shoved toward the objects that someone had
taken from me. (JANNINGS *looks away and* GEORGE *turns to*
PORTEN.) I was supposed to get them back myself.

PORTEN
(*Remembering*) Yes! How I fidgeted then!

VON STROHEIM

(*While looking away, speaks to* JANNINGS, *who is clearing his throat.*) You were about to say something?

JANNINGS

No.

(*Pause.*)

GEORGE

How strange! (*With this exclamation he wants to call attention to himself, but no one turns to him. Instead,* PORTEN *winks at* JANNINGS, *who thereupon puts a finger to his lips and shakes his head.* VON STROHEIM *then bends forward and elongates an eye with one finger. This time attention is paid to the sign: as a reply* JANNINGS *pulls his mouth apart with two fingers; thereupon* VON STROHEIM *turns up the lapel of his jacket by grasping it conspicuously with thumb and little finger, and* JANNINGS *nods twice.* PORTEN, VON STROHEIM, *and* JANNINGS *laugh.*) Strange!

PORTEN

(*Asks him almost reluctantly*) What's strange?

GEORGE

(*Relieved*) Suddenly I remembered a hill I had climbed with someone and the cloud shadows that appeared and vanished.

PORTEN

And what's strange about that?

GEORGE

That I should remember it so spontaneously.

PORTEN
(*Cleans her eye as if he had spit at her during his discourse. Very hostile*) Put your paper there away.

GEORGE
It's not my paper.

PORTEN
(*Snaps the paper away.*) And move your cup away from there. (*She snaps her fingers against the cup so that it turns over.*)

GEORGE
It isn't my cup.

PORTEN
And spare me your recollections. (*She instantly continues kindly to* VON STROHEIM) Do you know the expression "To mention the noose in the house of the man who's been hanged"?

(JANNINGS *laughs*, VON STROHEIM *smiles.*)

GEORGE
Why are you so hostile?

PORTEN
And why are you so pale?

GEORGE
I'm not pale!

PORTEN
And I'm not hostile! (*She continues at once.*) Do you know the expression "To place one's hands on one's head"?

GEORGE
(*Looks at* JANNINGS; *then replies.*) Certainly.

PORTEN
Why do you look at *him* before answering?

GEORGE
It's a habit.

PORTEN
Put your hands on your head. (*He hesitates.*) Did you hear what I said?

GEORGE
(*Again first looks at* JANNINGS.) I'm still thinking about it.

PORTEN
But the expression exists, doesn't it?

(GEORGE *slowly places his hands on his head.*)

VON STROHEIM
(*Is playing along.*) Put your hands on the table.

GEORGE
(*Tests whether the sentence exists.*) "Put your hands on the table." (*Relieved*) Yes. (*He puts his hands on the table.*)

PORTEN
Make your hands into fists and caress me!

GEORGE
(*Tests the sentence.*) "Make your hands into fists and caress me!?" No!

VON STROHEIM
Hand me the cup.

(GEORGE *hands him the cup unthinkingly.*)

PORTEN
I'll show you something (*She smiles at* VON STROHEIM *as her initiate and starts searching in her clothes. Eventually* GEORGE *stretches out his hand while she is still looking. Now and then she looks at his hand and continues to search. Suddenly she hits his hand and shoves it away. Maliciously*) That's what I wanted to show you.

(*He writhes and draws in his head. All at once she covers her eyes with both hands and shudders.*)

GEORGE
(*Startled*) What's the matter?

PORTEN
(*Takes her hands from her eyes.*) Oh, it's nothing. (GEORGE *wants to reach for the cup that* VON STROHEIM *has put down in the meantime, but* VON STROHEIM *displaces it a little and* GEORGE *withdraws his hand. They repeat this maneuver several times, both displaying a lot of patience.* PORTEN *interrupts the game; very hostile to* GEORGE) Who are you? (GEORGE *gets up quickly and assumes a pose behind the table as if his picture were about to be taken.*) Now I remember. You're the salesman. You gave me the . ·. (*She puts the riding crop on the table. She makes a slip of the tongue.*) How much is it?

GEORGE
Riding crop.

PORTEN
Yes, that's want I wanted to ask too. You sold me the riding crop.

(GEORGE *sits down,* PORTEN *again puts her hands over her eyes and shudders. She pushes the riding crop away.*)

JANNINGS
Don't you like it any more?

PORTEN
No, I only pushed it away.

JANNINGS
(*In a disguised voice*) The *riding crop* on the table, that means: someone who's very close to you will be swallowed up by a swamp and you will stand there slowly clapping your hands above your head. (*He laughs in a strange voice.* PORTEN *gets up quickly, pushing the guitar off the table in the process.* JANNINGS *in a disguised voice*) A *guitar* falls off the table, that means: hats staggering into glacial fissures during the next mountain-climbing expedition. (*He laughs in a strange voice.*)

VON STROHEIM
(*To* PORTEN, *who is standing motionless*) You want to leave?

PORTEN
(*Sits down.*) No, I stood up just now. (*She suddenly crosses her arms over her breast and hunches her shoulders.*)

GEORGE
Are you cold?

PORTEN
(*Drops her arms.*) No. (*To* VON STROHEIM) And who are you? (VON STROHEIM *picks up the guitar and holds it as he*

did previously. PORTEN *tenderly*) Oh, it's you! (*She becomes serious again immediately.*)

VON STROHEIM
Did you remember something?

(*Helplessly, she tries to give him another affectionate look, stops, reaches for a cigar.*)

GEORGE
Are you restless?

PORTEN
(*Puts the cigar back in the box. Serene*) No, I only wanted to take a cigar. (*Suddenly she screams*) I only wanted to take a cigar! (GEORGE *shies back, pulls his jacket over the head, as if he were protecting himself against rain, and stays hunched up like that.* PORTEN *screams*) I only wanted to take a cigar! I ONLY WANTED TO TAKE A CIGAR!

(*They all hunch up more and more. Now one hears a noise emanating from backstage, a high-pitched, pathetic howling.*
The howling coincides with a slight darkening onstage. PORTEN *immediately stops and hunches up too.*
The WOMAN WITH THE SCARF *steps swiftly out of the wings and walks to the second tapestry door without looking at anyone. As soon as she opens the door, there is quiet behind it. Instead, one hears the rustling of a newspaper, which is lying just inside the door. The* WOMAN *goes inside and returns with a big* DOLL *that represents a* CHILD. *The* CHILD *is quiet now, it has the hiccups. It is wearing a gold-embroidered white nightgown and looks very true to life. The mouth is enormous and open. As the* WOMAN *reaches center stage with the* CHILD, *it starts to bawl terribly, somehow without any preliminaries.* GEORGE, *jacket over his head, quickly leaps toward the chest and closes the drawer. The bawling stops at once.*

The WOMAN *carries the* CHILD *now from one to the other very fast, and in passing, during brief stops, it reaches for the women's breasts and between the men's legs. Very rapidly it also wipes off all the things that had been lying on the table, then pulls away the lace tablecloth and drops it. When the* WOMAN *stands with the* CHILD *beside* BERGNER, *who seems to be still asleep, it begins to bawl again, and as suddenly as if it had never stopped. The* WOMAN *holds it in such a way that the* CHILD *sees* BERGNER *from the front. It stops bawling at once and is carried away.*

The WOMAN *returns alone, closes the tapestry door, and goes off. After she has gone, they all sit there motionless. One of them tries to reach for something, but stops as soon as he starts. Someone else tries a gesture that atrophies instantly. A third wants to reply with a gesture, interrupts it twitching. They squat there, start to do something simultaneously; one of them futilely tries to pull his hand out of a pocket; one or two of them even open their mouths—a few sounds, then all of them grow stiff again and cuddle up, make themselves very small as if freezing to death.*

Only BERGNER *sits there the whole time motionless, with eyes closed. All of a sudden, as though she were playing "waking up," she moves slightly. By and by, the others look toward her.* VON STROHEIM *gets up and bends down to her. She again moves a little. The others are motionless. She opens her eyes and recognizes* VON STROHEIM; *she begins to smile.*)

The stage becomes dark.

Translated by Michael Roloff

They Are Dying Out

*"It suddenly occurs to me that I am
playing something that doesn't even
exist, and that is the difference. That is
the despair of it."*

Characters

HERMANN QUITT
HANS, *his confidant*
FRANZ KILB, *minority stockholder*
HARALD VON WULLNOW
BERTHOLD KOERBER-KENT   *businessmen and friends*
KARL-HEINZ LUTZ   *of* QUITT
PAULA TAX
QUITT'S WIFE

Act I

A large room. The afternoon sun is shining in from one side. The distant silhouette of a city, as though it were seen through a huge window, is visible in the background. (The background might also be formed by a backdrop, similar to a movie screen, with the silhouette of the city vaguely outlined against it.)

QUITT, wearing a sweat suit, is working out on a punching bag, belaboring it with his fists, feet, and knees. HANS, his confidant, wearing tails, stands next to him with a tray and a bottle of mineral water, watching. QUITT takes a sip from the bottle, pours some on his head, and sits down on a stool.

QUITT
I feel sad today.

HANS
So?

QUITT
I saw my wife in a dressing gown and her lacquered toes and suddenly I felt lonely. It was such a no-nonsense loneliness

/ 165

that I have no trouble speaking about it now. It relieved me,
I crumbled, melted away in it. The loneliness was objective,
a quality of the world, not something of myself. Everything
stood with its back to me, in gentle harmony with itself.
While I was taking a shit I heard the sounds I was making as
if they came from a stranger in the next cubicle. When I took
the bus to the office—

HANS
So as to maintain contact with the people and to study their
needs. For the purpose of R and D?

QUITT
—the sad curve which the bus described at one point at a
wide traffic circle cut like a yearning dream deep into my
heart.

HANS
The world's sorrow
Cut Mr. Quitt's feelings
To the marrow.
Hold on to your senses, Mr. Quitt. Someone as wealthy as
you can't afford these moods. A businessman who talks like
that, even if he really feels like that, is only giving a campaign
speech. Your feelings are a luxury and are useless. They might
be useful to those who could live according to them. Mr.
Quitt: for example, why don't you make *me* a gift of the
sorrows from your leisure time to reflect about my work. Or—

QUITT
Or?

HANS
Or become an artist. You're already supporting violin recitals;
you even condescended to collect money in public for the

acquisition of a painting by the National Gallery. The wealth of feelings that is yours as of any given date this month is not only useful but is even essential for an artist. Why don't you paint the curve, the curve of yearning which your bus described, on canvas? Why don't you sell your experience as a painting?

QUITT
(*Stands up.*) Hans, you're playing your daily role as if you knew it by rote. More realistically, please! More lovingly! Grander!

HANS
And the way Mr. Quitt just stepped out of his role—was that pure make-believe too?

QUITT
Let's not start splitting hairs. I admit: the salesgirl in the aforementioned bus eating French fries that smelled of rancid oil ruined my feelings—well, I would have loved to have slapped her face. On the other hand: shortly afterwards I met a black on the street; he was completely absorbed in the photos he'd just picked up from the drugstore, grinning to himself, swept away in remembrance, so that I suddenly remembered along with him, I felt solidarity with him. You're laughing. But there are moments when one's consciousness, too, takes a great leap forward.

HANS
But brutal reality
In no time destroys
That sense of solidarity.
However, I am laughing because you told me many times how you like to remember the time when you lived for days on end in Paris on nothing but French fries and ketchup.

QUITT

I had guests when I was telling that story. And in company, I sometimes also mention "the wood anemones and the hazelnut bushes from the springtime of my youth."

HANS

Does the addition of these artistic elements facilitate negotiations?

QUITT

Yes: by serving as an allegory for what is being left unsaid. The wood anemones beneath the hazelnut bushes then signify something altogether different. Only those who speak know that. The poetic element is for us a manifestation of the historic element, even if it is only a convention. Without poetry we would be ashamed of our deals, would feel like primordial man. By the way, just who exactly is coming today?

HANS

Harald von Wullnow
Karl-Heinz Lutz
Berthold Koerber-Kent
Paula Tax
all of them businessmen and friends of Quitt.

QUITT

I still have to change. If my wife comes, tell her to take care of the guests—then we can be sure that she'll go "bargain hunting" instead of flushing the toilet the whole time. Incidentally, I feel genuinely sad. Almost a comfortable feeling. (*Exit.*)

HANS

How easily Mr. Quitt talks about himself! You have to envy him his sadness. He becomes talkative then, like someone who's being filmed. In any event, time passes more quickly with a sad Quitt, because when he feels good he is distant, unapproachable, rubs his hands together briskly, hops up and down once, that's his Rumpelstiltskin act. (*He sits down on the stool.*) And what about me? What was I allowed to feel this morning? Isn't it true that you can tell more stories about yourself when you've just woken up than at any other time? Thus: the sun rose and shone into my open mouth. I hadn't had any dreams. I even find it repulsive the way people purse their mouth when they say "dream." When I brushed my teeth my gums bled. I would have liked to do it. But there was nothing doing. I: made a list of the meat to be ordered. Who am I, where did I come from, where am I going? Me . . . Yes, me, me! Always me. Why not someone else? (*He reflects and shakes his head.*) I have to try it when I'm with people. (*He gets up.* MINORITY STOCKHOLDER KILB *appears in the background.*) I can't remember anything personal about myself. The last time anyone talked about me was when I had to learn the catechism. "Your humble servant" of "Your Grace." Once I had a thought but I forgot it at once. I'm trying to remember it even now. So I never learned to think. But I have no personal needs. Still, I can indulge in a few gestures. (*He raises his fist but pulls it down again at once with the other hand. Now he notices* KILB.) Who are you, where did you come from, and so forth?

KILB
My name is Franz Kilb. (HANS *laughs.*) Don't you like the name?

HANS
It's something else. I was talking to myself just now—fluently almost. We don't have anything against names here. And *what* are you?

KILB
A minority stockholder.

HANS

The minority stockholder, perhaps?

KILB

Yes, *the* minority stockholder, Franz Kilb, the terror of the boards of directors, the clown of the stockholders' meetings, the tick in the navel of the economy with the nuisance value of 100—it's me, perking up again. (HANS *steps forward and puts one fist in front of* KILB's *face while showing him out with the other hand.*) Are you serious?

HANS

(*Steps back and drops his arms.*) I'd like to be. But I'm only serious when Mr. Quitt is serious. Nonetheless: it is my honor—scram! (KILB *sits down on the stool.*) So now you're going to tell us the story of your life, is that it?

KILB

I own one share of every major corporation in the country. I travel from one stockholders' meeting to the next and spend the nights in my sleeping bag. I go by bike—see, look at the trouser clips. I'm a bachelor in the prime of life, my reflexes function perfectly. (*He strikes his kneecap and his foot hits* HANS.) This is my Boy Scout knife; during the Second World War I passed my lifeguard test, I can pull you out of the water with my teeth. There are people who hold me in high esteem, but I don't put my name on any political endorsements. I once appeared on *What's My Line?*, I said I was self-employed, no one guessed what I did. At stockholders' meetings I sit with my rucksack and keep my hand up all the time. Stockholders' meetings where the board ignores someone who asks for the floor are null and void. How quiet it is here. Can you hear how quietly I am speaking? My last mistress called me demonic, the press (*He quickly proffers a few newspaper clippings.*) calls me a gadfly. I am quicker than you think. (*He has tripped up* HANS, *who has fallen on his knees.*) I live from my dividends and am a free person, in every respect. My motto is: "Anyone who's for me gets nothing from me; anyone against me will get to know me." That's a warning for you.

(QUITT *returns.* KILB *gets up at once, makes a bow, and steps into the background.*)

QUITT
The ubiquitous Mr. Kilb. (*To* HANS) Stop dusting your tails. As I was looking in the mirror while changing, it struck me as ridiculous that I was growing hair. These insensitive, indifferent threads. I was sitting on the bed, my head in my hands. After some time, I thought: If I keep holding my head like that, all my thoughts will cease. Besides, I really moved myself when I and my sadness regarded the blanket that I had thrown back in the morning. I will prove to you that my feelings are useful.

HANS
Watch out, if you say it once more, you'll suddenly even believe it. But seriously, I've never heard of a mad businessman. Only the other-directed find themselves ominous. But you're incapable of being at odds with the world. And if you are, you manage to make a profit at it.

QUITT
You're becoming schematic, Hans.

HANS
Because I'm a compulsive talker.

KILB
Ask him about his parents. His father was an itinerant actor. His mother made dolls which she couldn't sell. Both of them failed to return from a trip around the world. They're supposed to have jumped into a volcano. He's their only child.

QUITT
(*To* HANS) I'm not sick. Let's talk about something more
harmless.

(*Pause.*)

KILB
For example, the immortality of the soul?

(*Pause.*)

QUITT
The reason I'm not sick is because I, Hermann Quitt, can
be just the way I feel. And I'd like to be the way I feel. I
feel like the blues, Hans. (*Pause.*) In any event, sometimes
I go somewhere and I think I've come in through the wrong
door. Another second and they'll ask me who I am. Or I
suddenly stand on an incline in my empty office, see the
pencil roll down from the desk top and the papers slide off.
Even when I come in here, I often become afraid that I've
intruded. Frequently when I look at a familiar object I
think: Where's the trick? People I've known for ages I suddenly call by their last name. That's not just an old dream.
But I wanted to talk about something else. (*Pause.* KILB
raises his hand. QUITT *has suddenly butted his head against
the punching bag.*) What's still possible? What's there left
for me to do? Recently I drove through a suburban street
where I used to walk every day. Suddenly I saw an old board
for posters. In those days I used to look it over and read
everything on it. Now the board was nearly empty, only one
poster left, an ad for a powdered milk that's long off the
market. (*He raises his arms.*) As I drove slowly past, the
posters of all the bygone chocolates, toothpastes, and elec-
tions passed before my mind's eye, and in this gentle moment of recollection I was overcome by a profound sense of
history.

KILB and HANS
(*Simultaneously*) And then you palled it up with your chauffeur?

(*Pause. Honking offstage.*)

QUITT
That's Lutz. He also honks that way at night when he comes home. It's a signal for his wife to turn on the microwave oven. Made in Japan. Go help him with his coat.

(HANS *exits.*)

KILB
(*Steps forward.*) How does that story about your parents go?

QUITT
It's not idiotic enough. I once dreamed I was losing my hair. Whereupon someone told me that I was afraid of becoming impotent. But perhaps it only meant that I was afraid of losing my hair.

KILB
But why are you afraid of losing your hair? What does that mean? Besides, I caught sight of you recently. You were sitting on a bench by the river, rather absentmindedly engrossed in nature.

QUITT
Absentmindedly?

KILB
You hadn't even wiped the pigeon shit off the bench. Besides, experience tells me that the contemplation of nature is the first sign of a waning sense of reality. And your eyelids scarcely blinked, like a child's.

QUITT

Oh, go on, go on. It's beautiful to hear a story about oneself.

KILB

I went to have lunch. Steak and French fries. After all, I exist too.

QUITT

Kilb, I've admired you for a long time. I like your ruthlessness. That time when you brought an effigy of me to the stockholders' meeting and hung it on the lectern! And had yourself carried bodily out of the hall! I envy you too. Next to you I feel constricted, caught inside my skin, and notice how limited I am. I can tell you this now because it's just the two of us.

(KILB *draws* QUITT *forward by both ears and smacks a kiss on his lips.* QUITT *gives him a kick.*)

KILB

So as to re-establish the previous state of affairs. (*He retreats.*)

(*Simultaneously* HANS *leads* LUTZ, VON WULLNOW, *and* KOERBER-KENT *into the room.* KOERBER-KENT, *a businessman-priest, represents a Catholic-owned company; he is dressed in a suit, but wears the collar of his profession.*)

LUTZ

(*To his colleagues*) As I said, we weren't the first ones. We just observed them in the beginning, let them overextend themselves; then we got the green light from our overseas affiliates, tackled them, and down they went. He of course tried to bluff us, but we were on to him long ago. We let him twist in the wind a while longer and then we bagged him.

(*They laugh, each in his own way.*)

VON WULLNOW

(*To* QUITT) Quite something, that bike out there leaning against your fence. My father once gave me one almost like it, together with my first pair of knickers. They don't do work like that any more nowadays. Instead of selling you a bike, they dress it up like a machine, with speedometer and horn. And a machine of course is allowed to wear out more quickly than a simple bike. It is also characteristic of machines that they become obsolete. A bike wouldn't. Do you ride it to work? (QUITT *points to* KILB.) I wondered straight off why it was so dirty.

LUTZ

I'll take his arms. Who'll take the legs?

QUITT

And if we trip, the dragon seed falls out of his mouth. And the new Adam leaps to his feet.

KOERBER-KENT

He doesn't bother me. I find him entertaining. He reminds me of some dark urge inside myself. Besides, he doesn't really mean it. He can't help it, that's all. Ever since we had a chat, just the two of us, I believe him.

LUTZ

It's easy to believe someone if it's just the two of you. I believe anyone if it's just the two of us. But I get nothing out of it. That's why I try not to be alone with anyone. It falsifies the facts.

VON WULLNOW

He has no sense of honor, that s.o.b. He reminds me of an old nag we used to have at home. He pissed every time he stepped from his stall out on the pavement. It made such a wonderful splashing sound. He moved through the world with his joint dangling. And look how bowlegged he is. And the part in the middle of his hair—which isn't really centered. The threadbare fly, the pointy-toed shoes, that's no way to live!

KOERBER-KENT
Von Wullnow, you're wasting your time. There's no insulting him. Your elaborate insults only increase his self-esteem. Let's sit down and begin. I have to prepare a sermon today.

LUTZ
What are you going to preach on?

KOERBER-KENT
About the fact that death makes all men equal. Even us.

VON WULLNOW
(*Indicating* KILB.) He'd like that. But now—should he hear everything?

LUTZ
But we're not going to say anything that no one besides us should hear, are we?

(*Pause. The businessmen laugh.* KILB *is playing with his tongue in his mouth.* HANS *leaves. The businessmen sit down on a set of matching chairs and sofa.*)

VON WULLNOW
Are you standing comfortably, Kilb? We're only human, after all. (*The businessmen laugh again.* QUITT'S WIFE *appears. She looks at all of them, then walks diagonally through the room and disappears. To* KOERBER-KENT) Do you as a priest also employ female help in your enterprises?

KOERBER-KENT
How do you mean?

VON WULLNOW

I was just thinking about the fact that *you* aren't married, neither happily nor at all.

KOERBER-KENT

No, we can't marry.

VON WULLNOW

I didn't mean it that way.

QUITT

I don't understand your allusions.

VON WULLNOW

But you understand that they are allusions?

LUTZ

(*Distracting them.*) Of course, women are cheaper. But you have to be careful. Every month a few of them pull a fast one on us.

KOERBER-KENT

By pilfering inventory?

LUTZ

No, by becoming pregnant. Scarcely have they started work when they turn up with child—not out of passion, mind you, but out of cold calculation; and we have to pay the maternity benefits.

VON WULLNOW

One shouldn't always be talking about the good old days, but things *were* different in the past. You didn't even need to talk about the good old days then. Everyone was one big happy family in my grandfather's shop. They didn't work for my father, they worked for the shop, and that also meant for themselves—at least that's the feeling you got, and that's what mattered. Anyway, our system is the only one in which it is possible to work for oneself. It's incredible how strong my sense of solidarity was with my workers. It cut through all class differences and thresholds of natural feeling when they made their work easier for themselves by singing songs or urging each other on during particularly difficult jobs, with original chants which, incidentally, should be collected before they are forgotten altogether. Today they get the work over and done with, mutely and indifferently, that's all. Their thoughts are somewhere else, nothing creative any more, no imagination. I must say I admire our imports from the South. They're alive during their work, are happy to be together. Work is still part of their life for them. Moreover, in the good old days the workers used to take pride in their products; when they went for their Sunday walks they proudly pointed out to their children anything in the vicinity made by their own hands. Nowadays, most children haven't the faintest idea what their parents do at work.

KILB

Why, do you want them to point out the bolt in the car which their father personally screwed in, or the stick of margarine Mother wrapped herself?

VON WULLNOW

I don't have my cane with me. I refuse to touch you with my bare hands.

KOERBER-KENT

I recently had my library repapered. Of course, I helped with the work, and then I noticed the lack of enthusiasm with which the paper hangers were working, despite the fact that I was paying better than minimum wages. Why is it, I asked them, that you can't develop any passion for your work even

though you are paid for it? The good souls didn't have any
answer to that one.

VON WULLNOW
Typical.

(KILB *clipping his fingernails in the meantime.*)

KOERBER-KENT
They only think of the money. They've got nothing in their
minds except bread and broads, as I always put it. Instead of
enrolling in evening courses or absorbing our cultural herit-
age, they spend their wages on refrigerators, crystal, and
knickknacks. Since they no longer have any respect for the
public good—not to use a religious word in this circle—they
have become possessed by the devil of personal happiness, as
I sometimes say jokingly. And yet there's no way for them to
be personally happy without considering the public good.
You're scarcely born and already you're pushing into the re-
volving door of the here and now and can't push your way
back out, I always say. The paper wraps the stone, consump-
tion cracks the character.

VON WULLNOW
A story. No sermon without a little story, right? I know my
rhetoric. Which, incidentally, is another art that has gone to
the dogs among us . . . I was walking through the supermarket.

QUITT
You in a supermarket?

VON WULLNOW
Mine, of course. But I wanted to tell a story.

QUITT

Von Wullnow, the supermarket baron, that's news.

VON WULLNOW

I had to invest, taxes forced us to. I don't have to explain that to you. And besides, a big chain is just the right market for some of our products. That way we have our own outlets and don't need to discount to the retailers.

QUITT

"Harald Count von Wullnow Supermarkets."

VON WULLNOW

We called them Miller-Markets. Anyway, when I went to inspect one of them, I couldn't help noticing a woman who made herself conspicuous by standing around a long time with an empty shopping cart. I watched her and wondered to myself, because, aside from the furtive glances she was casting about, she seemed almost ladylike. Suddenly she came up to me and said softly, Do you think they still have the giant-size detergent on sale that was advertised last week? Too bad, I thought afterward. She was just my shirt size, I liked her layout. But to lose one's dignity over a consumer article like that! I felt quite ashamed for the person.

(KILB *has placed his hands underneath his armpits and is producing farting noises.*)

LUTZ

All I have to say against the consumers is that they aren't informed. Why don't they read the business sections in their papers which publicize the *Good Housekeeping* tests? Why don't they join the consumer councils? No wonder they can't tell the products apart. Did you ever watch the faces of house-wives during a sale? A mass of mindless, dehumanized, panic-stricken grimaces that don't even perceive each other any more, staring hypnotically at objects. No logic, no brains, nothing but the seething, stinking subconscious. A happening at the zoo, gentlemen. No awareness, no life, no feeling for quality. I know whereof I speak.

KILB
(*Interrupts them.*) Fire!

QUITT
(*Ignores him.*) And whereof are you speaking?

LUTZ
You know very well. We stopped production just now. Our quality product had no chance against your mass-produced one. Your brand is a household name, even our packaging, a three-dimensional picture on a hexagonal cover, was too revolutionary. Consumers are conservative, their curiosity about progress is fly-by-night. That was our first fire—I mean fiasco. (*Looks at* KILB.)

QUITT
When your product came on the market, I immediately put ours on the steal-me list.

KOERBER-KENT
Please explain.

QUITT
The steal-me list is a full-page ad which we publish once a week in the major newspapers. It lists the ten products of ours that are shoplifted with the greatest frequency. Simultaneously we send this list as posters to the trade. There they construct a kind of altar display of the listed objects and the poster with the legend SHOPLIFTERS' HIT PARADE is hung above it. This boosts sales. I immediately put my product at the top of the list and left it there, until Lutz gave up. I must say

I've grown fond of it in the meantime and look at it in its plain square package with genuine affection. Still, I'm going to stop production on it.

LUTZ
What do you mean?

QUITT
It was a losing proposition for a long time. I just didn't want you to get a swelled head.

VON WULLNOW
Marvelous, Quitt! That's the old school spirit, but I can see now how important it is that we reach an agreement in time.

QUITT
Otherwise why would you be here?

VON WULLNOW
Businessmen are people who get things moving, as Schumpeter says. Let's oil the machinery of the world.

KILB
Someone's coming.

VON WULLNOW
(*Doesn't hear him.*) This is an important day. For the first time we want to give up our atomization. We've been lonely long enough. We planned in loneliness, in sad isolation we watched the market, helplessly each of us set his price by himself, hoping for the best. Despising everything that was alien, each of us on his little island watched the other's advertising campaigns. We did not recognize our mutual needs, were even proud of our individualism. That has to change; we can't go on like this.

(PAULA TAX *hurriedly enters.*)

QUITT
I was just thinking of you, Paula.

PAULA
And?

QUITT
Nothing bad.

VON WULLNOW
Have a seat. (*To the others*) I always find it embarrassing to say to a woman, Sit down. (*To* PAULA) All of us were thinking of you. Even the Vicar-General, I think?

KOERBER-KENT
(*Jokingly*) Now I know why I felt the whole time as if a door had been left open somewhere.

KILB
Your signet ring is tarnished, Monsignore.

KOERBER-KENT
Continue, my friend. (KILB *remains silent.*) He's never got more than one sentence in him. The habit of quick interjections has ruined him.

(PAULA *has sat down. She is still wearing riding clothes.* QUITT'S WIFE *comes in again. She pretends she is looking for something.* PAULA *loosens her scarf and shakes her hair.* QUITT'S WIFE *stomps her feet. As she walks on, the heel of her shoe gets caught in a crack in the floor. She hops backward, slips back into the shoe, and tries to walk out with measured steps.* KILB *barks after her and she disappears with a scream.*)

QUITT

Perhaps the reason for the nausea is that only a minute ago you could have held an entirely different opinion of the matter, and in that case the story would have taken an entirely different turn.

PAULA

You look at me as if I should ask, What does this mean?

QUITT

Please remind me later that I must still explain something to you.

PAULA
When?

QUITT
Later.

LUTZ

I don't want to be pushy. There's a lot at stake today. I wouldn't have been able to fall asleep last night without my autogenic training. I usually think of the ocean when that happens, but even that sparkled for a long time like freshly mashed spinach from my new freezer package, and the moon above had been crossed out with a felt pen and a smaller one circled in beside it.

VON WULLNOW

All right, let's get down to business. I assume, if not our conversation, then what we mean by it is ears only. In any event, you have my word of honor. (*He takes a look around.*) The Vicar-General swears on this, doesn't he? Lutz promises, or no? And Quitt? Nods. Mrs. Tax's thoughts are still nudging her horse with her thighs. And our guest of honor? (*He nods briefly toward* KILB.)

QUITT
Hans.

(HANS *appears at once, frisks* KILB, *shakes his head—"no microphone"—and withdraws again.* KILB *thereupon takes his stool and sits down with the others, assumes the pose of a kibitzer.*)

VON WULLNOW
We're no sharks. But we've learned that free enterprise is a dog-eat-dog business. Public opinion regards us as monsters belching cigar smoke. And in the often so poetically quoted moments of those overly long cross-country trips we see ourselves like that: we've become what once we didn't want to become at any price. Don't shake your head, Vicar-General. You know that's not the way I mean it. No, we aren't just the bad guys in a game: we really are bad. Even as a gourmet, my face has slowly but surely become less and less soulful—although for a long time I hoped for the opposite. Just take a look at your colleagues business-lunching in the three-star restaurants, Lutz: their jowls register a lifelong sellout. A lifelong circus, not just twice a year like the housewives. Still, it is premature undialectical impressionism, as Mrs. Tax would surely say, trying to dump on us. After all, we didn't become monsters because we relished it. My primal experience is the thought: There's no such thing as a human being who becomes inhuman of his own accord. That's what I tell myself whenever I have to put myself together again after having done something I actually abhor in my heart of hearts.

QUITT
What you're trying to say is that it's futile to try to enlarge the market any further by means of price wars.

LUTZ

(*Glances at* KILB.) Not like that. Everyone should be able to translate it into his own terms.

QUITT

Competition is a game. Fighting is childish. Together we can underbid the small fry until they long to live from dividends. Not force, but the gentle law of displacement. When I was a child I would sometimes quietly sit down on something that someone else wanted, and absentmindedly whistle a song to myself.

KOERBER-KENT

You're not at confession here, Quitt.

QUITT

To the point: first of all: there are too many products, the market has become opaque. Who is producing too much? One of us? Perish the thought. Who then? They, of course. We're going to make the market transparent again. Second: now there are no longer too many products but too many units of the same product. The refrigeration plants are bursting with butter, I read at breakfast today. Is our supply too large? No, demand is too low, and that's the catch we live off of. Third of all: is demand too low because prices are too high? Of course. And prices are too high because wages are too high, right? So we are going to have to pay lower wages. But how? By having the work done more cheaply somewhere else. Say, "Mauritius represents an excellent labor market. The plantations have accustomed the population to hard work for generations. The nimble Asiatic fingers have become skilled and are a proven value." Therefore, we will be able to claim that our merchandise is a bigger bargain. That's the biggest drawing card. Besides, imagine that all goods will bear the legend: "Made in Mauritius." I remember the yearning such labels used to instill in me as a child. Why shouldn't they exert the same effect on our beloved consumers? In any event, demand will rise and we will match up our prices again. Fourth: from time to time we take a walk through the forest by ourselves so as to feel like human beings. Fifth: (*To* VON WULLNOW) All this time I've felt the irresistible urge to wipe off your wet mouth. (*He wipes off* VON WULLNOW's *mouth with a handkerchief. To* KILB) Repeat what I've said just now.

(*Pause.*)

KILB

(*Moves his lips, falters, tries again, shakes his head. He hops on his stool toward* QUITT.) Anyway, it sounded logical. As logical as this here. (*He tugs at both his ears and his tongue sticks out of his mouth, grabs his chin, and the tongue slips back inside. The businessmen meanwhile have exchanged significant glances.*)

LUTZ
So we're celebrating already?

QUITT
I'm not finished yet.

KOERBER-KENT
What were you playing just now? It was just a game, wasn't it? Because in reality you are—

QUITT
(*Interrupts him.*) Yes, but only in reality. (*To* VON WULL-NOW) And you are speechless?

VON WULLNOW
I'm just getting used to you again. Perhaps you're just one of those people who like to squeeze other people's pimples.

QUITT

(*Strikes his forehead histrionically.*) True, I was carried away by something. But now I'm normal again.

VON WULLNOW

It passed so quickly I've already forgotten it. I was brushed by a bat. Did something happen? Besides, you haven't finished yet.

QUITT

What is important is that from now on none of us does anything without the other. When I buy raw materials without informing you of my source, that's treason. When Lutz brings a new product on the market to corner a share of the turf, that's treason. If the Vicar-General pays his female labor a lower scale than we do, because they are devout farm girls, and depresses prices, that's treason. If you, Paula, let your workers share in the profits and have to raise prices all by yourself, that's treason. (*To* VON WULLNOW) That's the way you want it, isn't it?

VON WULLNOW

Mrs. Tax would probably pose the counterquestion: But what if I let them share because I find it reasonable—say, to increase production?

QUITT

(*To* PAULA, *as if she had answered for herself*) It's not treason as long as you don't raise your prices without first consulting us. And as long as you and I have the same habits, you can't betray me. And now the champagne, Hans.

(*A cork pops backstage.* HANS *appears at once, carrying a tray with champagne glasses and a bottle which is still smoking. The ceremony of pouring the champagne.* QUITT *points ironically to the quality of the champagne and glasses, for*

example: "Dom Pérignon 1935, Biedermeier glasses, hand-
blown, notice the irregularities in the glass." *The group rises
to its feet, clinks glasses, drinks quietly, looking into each
other's eyes.* KILB *has not gotten up. While the others are
drinking he briefly laughs a few times without the others
paying him any heed. He pulls out his knife, turns it back
and forth, and lets it fall mumblety-peg fashion to the floor.
They look at him without interest. He puts the knife away
and plays a little on his harmonica.* HANS *has already left
with the tray.* KILB *gets up and spits at the feet of each person, one after the other. In front of* PAULA *he uses his hand
to pull out his chin, simultaneously sticking out his behind.
The rest continue to regard him benignly. Suddenly he picks
up* LUTZ *and the priest, who don't object, one after the
other, and puts them down somewhere else. He crisscrosses
the stage. In passing, he kicks them lightly on the backs of
their knees so that their legs give a little, except for the last
one. He offers* PAULA *his thigh, Harpo Marx fashion, which
she holds and then lets drop again; he makes an exception of*
QUITT, *only casting sidelong glances at him. Now he has also
begun to speak.*)

KILB

And I? Is it my job to take care of the entertainment? Am I
the critter whose ears are allowed to hear everything? Or the
poodle in front of whom you lie down naked in bed? I can
drag you across your beautiful lawns with my teeth. I'll stuff
the gaps in your beautiful whole sentences with pus. I'll cram
your spray-deodorized private parts into Baggies. You singe
the fluff off slaughtered chickens with a candle. In Switzer-
land they say "chicken skin" instead of "goose bumps." Enjoy!
Enjoy! I always speak this calmly, dear lady. Here, you've
dropped your Charmin. (*He pulls out a strip of toilet paper
and places it over her arm; she smiles, unimpressed.*) If you
ever catch fire it will be me who wraps you in blankets until
you choke to death. And when you all freeze to death I'll sit

beside you cracking my knuckles. Diabolical, don't you agree? (*More and more embarrassed*) Let yourselves be conjured up out of your personal hedgerows, you, the bewitched of the business world, a free man stands before you, a model, a picture-book figure. (*He slaps his hands together, slaps his thighs and the soles of his shoes like a folk dancer, only more slowly and awkwardly.*) Let's swing a little! Action! Lights! A little circus atmosphere! Not just words against which the brain is defenseless anyway! Conserve your vocal chords! More body language! (*He picks up a champagne glass and lets it drop somewhat helplessly, makes a vain reflex movement to catch it, which he tries to overplay.*) And don't stand around like a bunch of stiffs! Anyway, far too statuesque! Move. You will be recognized by your movements. Let's celebrate. (*He dances* PAULA *a few steps farther across the stage, then stops in front of her. He starts unbuttoning her blouse . . . He encourages himself by beating his fists together and blowing into the hollow of his hands. In between he sticks his hands into his armpits as if they were freezing. No one stops him. Sidelong glances at* QUITT. QUITT *watches him attentively as well as remotely, almost impatiently.* KILB *tugs the blouse out of the riding britches, somewhat indecisively.* PAULA *merely smiles. He steps back as if he were giving up, performs another pathetic slapping gesture without really slapping his hands together. Suddenly* QUITT *leaps forward, seizes* KILB's *hand, and wants to use it to tear off* PAULA's *blouse himself.* KILB *resists.* QUITT's WIFE *enters, watches with interest.* QUITT *lets go of* KILB *and tears off the blouse himself.* PAULA *crosses her arms in front of her breasts without undue hurry.* QUITT's WIFE *leaves.* QUITT *places another champagne glass in* KILB's *hand, simultaneously takes the other glasses into his fist, and smashes them, one after the other, on the floor, repeating* KILB's *words—*"Enjoy! enjoy!"—*while doing so . . . nudges him in the side until* KILB, *too, drops his glass, somewhat indecisively.* QUITT *walks from one person to the other and spits into each face; lifts up a splinter of glass and attacks* KILB *with it, throws the splinter away, and puts* KILB *into a headlock; leads him back and forth like this and butts his head against the others. In the headlock, trying to free himself)* You misunderstood me, Quitt. There's no method to your madness. It is unaesthetic, vulgar, formless. But worst of all, it is unmusical, has neither melody nor rhythm. That wasn't how we planned it. Don't you understand a joke? Can't you distinguish between ritual and reality any more? Know your limits, Quitt.

QUITT
(*While pushing him into a chair and dragging him offstage on it*) Until now you have lived off the fact that I have my limits, you phony. Now show me my limits, you model of the independent life. (*Far upstage he tips him out of sight and comes back.*)

(PAULA *walks off with measured steps.* HANS *reappears with a dustpan and whisk broom. The others are cleaning themselves. Everyone begins to smile.* QUITT *does not smile.* HANS *sweeps the splinters together.* PAULA *returns dressed and smiles also, with closed lips.*)

VON WULLNOW
I believe he's finally learned his lesson.

KOERBER-KENT
He'll never learn anything, He's got no memory. The jack-in-the-box merely uses the floor to propel himself. He doesn't forget because he doesn't remember anything. The horsefly lands on the very spot it's just been shooed away from. He doesn't think backward and forward like us who have a sense of history—as Mrs. Tax might say—he only has a good nose. I would call him a mere animal, an involuntary, fidgeting animal. The sparrows in the field, not by living, but by being

lived, are the divine principle. I can see him now on his bicycle animalistically rushing down the tree-lined avenues.

QUITT
Don't always look at me when you speak; I can't listen to you that way.

VON WULLNOW
It's a pity that there are no more tree-lined avenues. How sweet, for instance, the memory of the manor house at dawn—the house at the vanishing point of the two rows of chestnut trees, the windows reflecting darkly, only the dormers of the servants' quarters already lighted up; a hedgehog rustles in the dry leaves at our feet, the special stagnant air of that time of day when the sick go into themselves and die willingly, and a chestnut suddenly thuds down and bursts on the gun on our shoulder while we have turned around for one last look at our parents' house before we stalk cross-country to our hunting ground. Yes, a delicate being, our minority stockholder, as delicate as a thief when it comes to opening a drawer, as delicate as a murderer when it comes to handling a knife.

LUTZ
Von Wullnow, your language is so elevated it makes me hesitate to tell my joke now.

VON WULLNOW
I order you to. You've been looking all this time as if you had something to get off your chest.

LUTZ
Two people love each other. They make love so rapidly, the way you sometimes devour a slice of bread with honey on it. When they are finished—(*Glances at* PAULA.) Oh, pardon me.

VON WULLNOW

Mrs. Tax isn't listening anyway. And besides, she's above that sort of thing. She'd probably consider our dirty jokes as proof of our commercialized sexuality, wouldn't you? Go on.

LUTZ

—the man gets up at once. Oh, says the woman, you've scarcely finished and you're already leaving? And that's supposed to be love? Look, the man replies, I counted to ten, didn't I?

(*There's either brief laughter or there isn't.* VON WULLNOW *is already in the process of departing with* LUTZ *and* KOERBER-KENT—*only* HANS, *who is still sweeping up broken glass, giggles, kneeling on the floor. The gentlemen turn around toward him; he gets up and proceeds out in front of them, giggling.*)

VON WULLNOW

Quitt, we trust you as you trust us. Forget your superannuated sensitivity. Sensitive for me is a word I only associate with condoms.

QUITT

(*To* PAULA) Aren't you leaving?

PAULA

I was to remind you that you still wanted to explain something to me.

QUITT

I merely *wished* you would stay, now you can go. (*Pause.* PAULA *sits down again. Pause.*) I noticed how I happened to think of you disgustingly by chance. One minute before and all I could have attached to you was your name. Suddenly there was something conspicuous about you. I wanted to get up and grab you between the legs.

PAULA

Are you speaking about me or about a thing?

QUITT

(*Laughs briefly. Pause.*) Just now I almost said: About you, you thing. Something seems to want to slip out of me today, something I'm afraid of but which still tantalizes me. You know the stories about laughing at funerals. Once I sat opposite a woman I didn't know. We looked into each other's eyes until I felt hot. Suddenly she stuck out her tongue at me, not just mockingly, a little between her lips, but all the way to the root, with the whole face a gruesome grimace—as though she wanted to stick herself out at me. Ever since then I've felt like doing something like that myself. Usually I manage to do it only in my head, for just a moment. It starts with my wanting to undo someone's shoelaces who's walking by or pulling a hair out of his nose, and stops with the urge to unzip my fly in company.

PAULA

Shouldn't we talk about our arrangement instead?

QUITT

But I'm finally beginning to enjoy talking. I am speaking now. Before, my lips just moved. I had to strain my muscles to enunciate properly. My whole chin ached, the cheeks became numb. Now I know what I am saying.

PAULA

Are you Catholic?

QUITT

Why! You're actually listening to me!

PAULA

Because you're talking about yourself like the deputy of universal truth. What you experience personally you want to experience for all of us. The blood you sweat in private you bring as a sacrifice to us, the impenitent ones. Your ego wants to be more than itself, your sentimentality appeals to my inability to feel, your urge to confess merely has the effect of demonstrating to me that I'm still unawakened. You behave as though your time had finally come. Actually, your time as Quitt who suffers his life in exemplary bourgeois fashion has long since passed. Your suffering is over. The fact that you insist so much on yourself makes you suspect. You lack a sense of history, you're much too much of an example of Western civilization for me.

QUITT

But even if it is for the last time, I'd like to be at the center of things, just by myself. Otherwise I would feel written off once and for all, like a machine, wouldn't be able to utter a single word meant for someone else. Once when I stepped out of the house the children yelled after me: I know who you are! I know who you are! Tauntingly, as though the fact that I could be identified was something bad. Besides, it seemed inappropriate to me just now to tell something like a story after you thought about me in such abstract terms.

(*Pause.*)

PAULA

Sit down. (QUITT *does so. Pause. They look at each other.* PAULA *looks away.*) Yes, my outfit bothers me too now. And I can't think of anything I'd like to say to you. But I would like to say something to you. (*Pause.*) It's pleasant to sit here in the twilight. I wasn't thinking of anything just now. That was nice too. (*Pause.*) Do you like evaporated milk? I suddenly feel like having evaporated milk. (*Pause. She*

speaks as if she wants to avoid speaking of something else.)
My workers should never see me like this. Normally, I buy
my clothes ready-to-wear, I even feel good in them. By the
way, it occurred to me before that we should also plan our
advertising together from now on. I would like to go on the
basis that we don't generate any artificial needs but only
awaken the natural ones of which people aren't conscious
yet. Most people don't even know their needs. Advertising,
insofar as it describes a product, is only another word for
consciousness-raising. What we should avoid is advertising
which is inappropriate to its product because it creates mis-
conceptions among the consumers about the nature of the
product. That would be the very deception or simulation of
something that isn't there which we are always accused of.
But our products exist and their very existence makes them
rational—otherwise we, as rational beings, would not have
had them produced in a rational manner from rational raw
materials by rational people. And if our advertisements don't
lie but only provide an exact description of our rational products, then the advertising will be just as rational. Take a look
at the socialist states. They have no irrational products—and
still they advertise, because the rational needs advertising
most of all. That's what transmits the idea of what is rational.
For me advertising is the only materialistic poetry. As an
anthropomorphic system it endears us to the objects from
which we have been alienated by ideology. It animates the
world of goods and humanizes them, so that we can feel at
home with them. I can't tell you how deeply touched I am
when I read on an old fire wall in giant letters PEPSI-COLA
HITS THE SPOT. When I see a detergent container in front of
a rising sun, it blows my mind. Today, twenty years later,
they simply gave the same product the sappy designation
IT'S THE PEPSI GENERATION, and my mind goes blank. When
I'm feeling unproductive, I look at ads in magazines, it makes
my mood seem ridiculous; so advertising is also a form of
consolation, but of a concrete, rational kind, as distinct from

bourgeois obscurantist poetry. And think with how much more dignity and how much more progressively the copywriters can work than the poets! While the poets in their isolation conjure up something vague, the copywriters, working as an efficient team, describe the definite. Indeed, they are the only truly creative ones—they think something they had no idea about beforehand. Incidentally, we noticed recently what was wrong with the slogan for one of our products. It contained the phrase "a level tablespoon" and the product didn't sell. Finally it occurred to one member of the team to substitute the word "heaping" for small. Instead of "level tablespoon" we used "a heaping teaspoon," and suddenly sales increased by almost 100 percent.

(HANS *enters during the last sentence and turns on the light.*)

QUITT
(*To* HANS) We don't need any light.

(HANS *turns off the light and leaves.*)

PAULA
I can hear my wristwatch ticking.

QUITT
You should be able to afford a noiseless watch. But that probably is an heirloom, not just any old watch. So please try to remember. (*Pause.*) Or don't try to remember—as you please.

PAULA
If you tell a child who is singing to itself: Very nice, go on singing! it will stop singing. But if you say: Stop! it will go on singing.

QUITT
There are women who—

PAULA
Stop it, nothing can come of that.

QUITT
There are women you can't touch because if you did you would be desecrating an heirloom. A necklace, then, has a story which makes every caress of the neck a mere afterthought. Everything about the woman is so complete that every experience you share with her only reminds her of something in her past. Whatever you tell her, she immediately interrupts you with this introverted nodding of the head. She is untouchable, inside and out. She is so full of memories. The most mysterious, delicately stuttering impulse immediately evokes a doppelgänger who has already made the impulse crystal-clear to the woman. You begin to understand sex killers: only the slitting open of the belly provides him with the attention every individual deserves. You can't run your hands through a hooker's hair—so that her hairdo won't get messed up.

PAULA
It's just as you say it is. But why is it like that? Who is responsible for that? And who makes sure that it stays that way? And who profits by it? Instead of naming the causes, you make fun of their appearances. And precisely that happens to be one of the causes. To describe pure appearances is a man's kind of joke. Von Wullnow would say that I would say: undialectical impressionism.

QUITT
And you: because you've got so many causes on your mind, you forget to bother with the appearances. Instead of appearances, you see nothing but causes. And when you elimi-

nate the causes so as to change the appearances, they have already changed so that you have to eliminate entirely different causes. And if you look at me now, please become aware of me for once and not my causes.

PAULA
You have a beautiful tie pin. Your shirt is so new that one can still see the pinholes. Your grinding jaws manifest will power. Your delicate hands might be those of a pianist. One of your earlobes has dried shaving cream on it. And while you behave animalistically, the creases on your pants give you away.

(QUITT *gets up and pulls* PAULA *toward him. She wraps her arms exaggeratedly around him and also puts one leg around his hip, throws back her head, and sighs derisively. He lets go of her at once and walks away. She walks backward. They pursue each other alternately for a short time. Then they walk around by themselves, finally stop.*)

QUITT
Please stop being conceptual. I once gave someone a present, some chocolate for his child. The chocolate was wrapped in small squares, each one with a picture of a different fairy-tale motif. Oh, the father said disappointedly, it's not a puzzle! And then he said: That's it, deprivation of the imagination by the chocolate manufacturers. When he said that, I suddenly stood very distantly beside him and felt radically alone. I looked down at the floor in utter loneliness. So, please stop.

PAULA
But you were the one who started it.

QUITT
Do you see that nail sticking out of the wall there?

PAULA
Yes.

QUITT
It's long, isn't it?

PAULA
Very long.

QUITT
And how thick is your head?

(*Pause.*)

PAULA
Perhaps I should turn on the light after all.

(*Pause.*)

QUITT
Today the doorbell rang. Because I was curious who it was, I went to open the door myself. It was only the eggman, whom the so-called estate sends around from house to house once a week. He always comes at the same time. I'd forgotten. "Can't you be someone else for once?" I wanted to scream.

(*Pause.*)

PAULA
And what if *I* were someone else?

(QUITT *takes one step toward her. She does not step back.*)

QUITT
And recently I saw a silent film. No music had been dubbed in, so it was almost completely quiet in the theater. Only

now and then when something funny happened a few scattered children laughed and stopped again at once. Suddenly I had a sense of death. The feeling was so strong that I yanked my legs far apart and spread my fingers. What social conditions can you use to explain that? Does this syndrome already bear someone's name? If so, whose?

PAULA
I can't explain it to you by social conditions. It is unconditionally yours and can't be emulated. As a social factor it's not worth mentioning. The masses have other worries.

QUITT
But which will pass.

PAULA
Yes, because the conditions will pass too.

QUITT
And then the masses will perhaps have my worries, which do not pass.

(WIFE *appears with a magazine in her hand.*)

WIFE
Austrian dramatist, dead, seven letters?

QUITT
Nestroy.

WIFE
No.

QUITT
Across or down?

WIFE
Across.

QUITT
Raimund.

WIFE
Of course. (*Exits.*)

(*Pause.*)

PAULA
The watch—it isn't an heirloom. (*Pause.*) Is that still too conceptual?

QUITT
Now I won't tell you what I'm thinking.

PAULA
And what are you thinking?

QUITT
It's kind of you to ask. But why don't you ask me of your own volition? I yearn to be questioned by you. Do I have to bang my head against the floor to make you ask about me? (*He throws himself on the floor and actually bangs his head a few times against it, then stands up at once and steps up to* PAULA.) I would like to snap at the world now and swallow it, that's how inaccessible everything seems to me. And I too am inaccessible, I twist away from everything. Every event I could possibly experience slowly but surely transforms itself back into lifeless nature, where I no longer play a role. I can stand before it as I do before you and I am back in prehistory without human beings. I imagine the ocean, the fire-spewing volcanoes, the primordial mountains on the horizon, but the conception has nothing to do with me. I don't even appear

dimly within it as a premonition. When I look at you now, I see you only as you are, and as you are entirely without me, but not as you were or could be with me; that is inhuman.

PAULA

Excuse me, but I can't concentrate any longer. (*She takes a step, so that their bodies touch.*) So what were you thinking?

(*Pause.*)

QUITT

You know it anyway.

PAULA

Perhaps. But I'd like to hear you say it.

QUITT

Now I feel strong enough not to tell you any more.

PAULA

(*Steps back.*) We are alone.

QUITT

I am alone and you are alone, not we. I would not want to transpose the "we" of our deal to you and me at this moment.

PAULA

Isn't this moment, too, part of our deal?

QUITT

Don't you get out of your box even for a second?

PAULA

Your impatience is what keeps me boxed in.

QUITT
(*Flings her to the floor. She lies there, supports herself on one elbow. Then she gets up.*) How gracefully you get back on your feet!

PAULA
I'd like to leave now.

QUITT
Hans!

(HANS *appears with a long fur coat over his arm and first walks in the wrong direction.*)

QUITT
Over here. Where did you think you were?

HANS
(*Helps* PAULA *into her coat.*) Always with you, Mr. Quitt. It was bright in the room I just left.

PAULA
Hans, you're good at helping people into their coats.

HANS
Mrs. Quitt has the same one.

PAULA
(*To* QUITT) I would like to tell you something about myself, Quitt, just like this, without being asked to. And note that, for the first time, I'm speaking about myself. After your wife left I slowly exhaled. And while exhaling . . . please don't laugh.

QUITT
I'm not laughing.

PAULA
While exhaling . . . please don't laugh.

QUITT
Another second and I will.

PAULA
(*Loudly*) As I exhaled, love set in. (*She leaves.*)

QUITT
(*To* HANS) Don't say anything.

HANS
I'm not saying anything.

   (QUITT'S WIFE *enters, turns on mild indirect lighting, and
sits down. She gives* HANS *a signal to leave.*)

QUITT
Nobody's cleaned up. (HANS *proceeds to dust. To his* WIFE)
And what did you do all day?

WIFE
You saw what I did: I went in and out and back and forth.

QUITT
And what was it like in town?

WIFE
People respected me.

   (HANS *leaves.*)

QUITT
Was there anything new?

WIFE
I stole this blouse.

QUITT
The main thing is not to get caught. Anything else?

WIFE
I stopped here and there and then walked on. Why don't you sit down too?

QUITT
You don't look well.

(*Pause.*)

WIFE
Yes, but at least it's already evening. (*She gets up and walks out quickly.*)

(QUITT *sits down even before she's gone. He remains alone for a while. The silhouette of the city is completely illuminated in the meantime.* HANS *returns with a book.* QUITT *looks up.*)

HANS
It's me, still.

QUITT
Tell me, Hans, what's your life actually like?

(HANS *sits down.*)

HANS
I knew what you would say the moment you opened your mouth. But I couldn't interrupt you at that point. So let's forget it.

(*Pause.*)

QUITT
Stop looking me in the eye.

HANS
I do that whenever I'm at a loss how to please you.

QUITT
Tell me about yourself.

HANS
What do you mean?

QUITT
Don't you understand, I am curious to know your story. How do *you* behave when you would like to speak but can only scream? Don't you sometimes get so tired that you can only imagine everything flat on the ground? Doesn't it also sometimes happen to you that when you think of your relationship to others you only see heavy wet rags lying around everywhere? Now tell me about yourself.

HANS
You mention me.
Yourself you mean.

(*Pause.*)

QUITT
Why does my itty-bitty mind go yakking so affectedly into the big wide world? And can't help itself? (*Screams*) And doesn't want it any differently? I am important. I am important. I am important. Incidentally, why don't you look me in the eye now?

HANS
Because there's nothing new to see there.

(*Pause.*)

QUITT
Please read to me.

HANS
(*Sits down and reads.*) " 'I shall have to let you go after all,'
his uncle said one day at the end of the midday meal, just as
a magnificent thunderstorm was breaking, sending the rustling rain like diamond missiles down into the lake, so that
it twitched and seethed and heaved. Victor made no reply
whatever but listened for what else would come. 'Everything
is futile in the end,' his uncle started up again in a slow
drawn-out voice, 'it's futile, youth and old age don't belong
together. The years that could have been used have passed
now, they are lowering down on the other side of the mountains and no power on earth can drag them back to the near
side where cold shadows are already falling.' Victor could not
have been more awed. The venerable old man happened to
be sitting in such a way that the lightning flashes illuminated
his face, and sometimes, in the dusky room, it seemed as
though fire flowed through the man's gray hair and light
trickled across his weatherbeaten face. 'Oh, Victor, do you
know life? Do you know that thing that people call old
age?'—'How could I, Uncle, as I am still so young?'—'True,
you don't know it, and there's no way you could. Life is
boundless as long as you are still young. You always think you
still have a long stretch ahead of you, that you've traveled
only a short way. That's why you put so much off to the next
day, why you put this and that aside, to tackle it later on.
But then when you want to tackle it, it is too late and you
notice that you are old. That is why life is a limitless field if
you look at it from the beginning, and is scarcely two paces
long when you regard it from the end. It is a sparkling thing,
something so beautiful that you feel like plunging into it,
and you feel that it would have to last forever—and old age
is a moth darting in the dusk, fluttering ominously about
our ears. That is why you would like to stretch out your hands

so as not to have to leave, because you have missed so much. When an aged man stands on a mountain of achievements, what good is it to him? I have done much, all sorts of things, and have nothing from it. Everything turns to dust in a moment if you haven't built an existence that outlasts your coffin. The man who has sons, nephews, and grandsons around him in his old age will often become a thousand years old. Then the same many-sided life persists even when he is gone, life continues just the same; yes, you don't even notice that one small segment of this life veered off to the side and never came back any more. With my death everything that I myself have been will disappear.' After these words the old man stopped speaking. He folded his napkin together, as was his custom, rolled it into a cylinder, and shoved it into the silver ring which he kept for the purpose. Then he assembled the various bottles into a certain order, put the cheese and sweetmeats on their plates, and plunged the glass bells over them. Yet of all these objects he took none away from the table, as was his usual habit, but left them standing there and sat before them. Meanwhile, the thunderstorm had passed, with softer flashes and a muted thundering it moved down the far slope of the craggy eastern mountain range, and the sun fought its way back out, gradually filling the room with a lovely fire. At daybreak the next morning Victor took his walking stick into his hand and slung one strap of his satchel over his arm. The spitz, who understood everything, bounded with joy. Breakfast was consumed amid much small talk. 'I'll take you as far as the gate,' the uncle said when Victor had gotten up, had hitched his satchel on his shoulder, and was about to take his leave. The old man had gone into the adjacent room and must have triggered a spring or set off some kind of mechanical contraption; for at that moment Victor heard the rattling of the gate and saw, through the window, how that gate opened slowly by itself. 'Well,' said his uncle while walking out, 'everything is ready,' Victor reached for his walking stick and placed his cap on his head.

The uncle walked down the stairs with him and across the open space in the garden as far as the gate. Neither said a word during their walk. At the gate the uncle stopped. Victor looked at him for a while. Tears shimmered in his bright-colored eyes, testifying to a profound emotion—then he suddenly bent down and vehemently kissed the wrinkled hand. The old man emitted a dull uncanny sound like a sob—and pushed the youth out by the gate. In two hours the latter had reached Attmaning, and as he stepped out from the dark trees toward the town he happened to hear its bells tolling, and never has a sound sounded so sweet to him as this tolling which fell so endearingly upon his ears, a sound he had not heard for so long. The Innkeeper's Alley was filled with the beautiful brown animals of the mountains which the cattle dealers were driving down toward the lowland, and the inn's guest room was full of people since it was market day. It seemed to Victor as if he had been dreaming for a long time and had only now returned to the world. Now that he was back out in the fields of the people, on their highways, part of their merry doings, now that the expanse of gentle rolling hills stretched out wide and endless before him, and the mountains which he had left hovered behind as a blue wreath; now his heart came apart in this great circumambient view and outraced him far, far beyond the distant, scarcely visible line of the horizon . . ."

QUITT

How nice that this armchair has a headrest. (*Pause.*) How much time has passed since then! In those days, in the nineteenth century, even if you didn't have some feeling for the world, there at least existed a memory of a universal feeling, and a yearning. That is why you could replay the feeling and replay it for the others as in this story. And because you could replay the feeling as seriously and patiently and conscientiously as a restorer—the German poet Adalbert Stifter after all was a restorer—that feeling was really produced, perhaps.

In any event, people believed that what was being played there existed, or at least that it was possible. All I actually do is quote; everything that is meant to be serious immediately becomes a joke with me, genuine signs of life of my own slip out of me purely by accident, and they exist only at the moment when they slip out. Afterward then they are—well—where you once used to see the whole, I see nothing but particulars now. Hey, you with your ingrown earlobes! it suddenly slips out of me, and instead of speaking with someone whom I notice, I step on his heels so that his shoe comes off. I would so like to be full of pathos! Von Wullnow, with a couple of women bathing in the nude at sunrise, bawled out nothing but old college songs in the water—that's what's left of him. What slips out of me is only the raw sewage of previous centuries. I lead a businessman's life as camouflage. I go to the telephone as soon as it rings. I talk faster with the car door open behind me. We fix our prices and faithfully stick to our agreements. Suddenly it occurs to me that I am playing something that doesn't even exist, and that's the difference. That's the despair of it! Do you know what I'm going to do? I won't stick to our arrangement. I'm going to ruin their prices and them with it. I'm going to employ my old-fashioned sense of self as a means of production. I haven't had anything of myself yet, Hans. And they are going to cool their hot little heads with their clammy hands, and their heads will grow cold as well. It will be a tragedy. A tragedy of business life, and I will be the survivor. And the investment in the business will be me, just me alone. I will slip out of myself and the raw sewage will sweep them away. There will be lightning and thunder, and the idea will become flesh.

(*There is thunder.*)

HANS
This time
I can find no rhyme.

QUITT
Good night.

(HANS *leaves.* QUITT *drums his fists on his chest and emits Tarzan-like screams. Pause. His* WIFE *comes in and stops in front of him.*)

WIFE
I have something else to say to you.

QUITT
Don't speak to me. I want to get out of myself now. I am now myself and as such I am on speaking terms only with myself.

WIFE
But I would like to say something to you. Please.

(*Pause.*)

QUITT
(*Suddenly very tender*) Then tell me. (*He takes her around the waist, she moves in his embrace.*) Tell me.

WIFE
I . . . where it . . . because . . . hm (*She clears her throat.*) . . . and you . . . isn't it . . . (*She laughs indecisively.*) . . . this and that . . . and autumn . . . like a stone . . . that roaring . . . the Ammonites . . . and the mud on the soles of the shoes . . . (*She puts her hand to her face, and the stage becomes dark.*)

END ACT ONE

Act II

The silhouette of the city. The punching bag has been replaced by a huge balloon which, almost imperceptibly, is
shrinking. A large, slowly melting block of ice with a spot
shining on it has replaced the matching sofa and armchairs,
a glass trough with dough rising in it somewhere else, also
with a spot on it. A piano. A large boulder in the background
with phrases slowly and constantly appearing and fading on
it: OUR GREATEST SIN—THE IMPATIENCE OF CONCEPTS—THE
WORST IS OVER—THE LAST HOPE. Next to them are children's
drawings. The usual stage lighting (which remains the same
throughout).

HANS is lying on an old deck chair, dressed as before, and
is asleep. He is mumbling in his sleep and laughs; time
passes.

QUITT walks in from behind the wall, rubbing his hands.
He executes a little dance step while walking. He whistles to
himself.

QUITT

It's been ages since I've whistled! (*He hums. The humming makes him want to talk.*) Hey, Hans! (HANS *leaps up out of his sleep and immediately goes to relieve* QUITT *of the coat which he isn't wearing.*) You can't stop acting the servant even in your sleep, can you? When I was just singing to myself I suddenly couldn't stand being alone any more. (*He regards* HANS.) And now you're already annoying me again. Were you dreaming of me? Oh, forget it, I don't even want to know. (*He whistles again.* HANS *whistles along.*) Stop whistling. It's no fun if you whistle along.

HANS

I dreamed. Really, I was dreaming. The dream was about a pocket calendar with rough and smooth sides. The rough sides were the work days, the smooth ones the days which I have off. I slithered for days on end over calendar pages.

QUITT

Dream on, little dreamer, dream—just as long as you don't interpret your dreams.

HANS

But what if the dream interprets itself—as it did just now?

QUITT

You are talking about yourself—why is that?

HANS

You've infected me.

QUITT

And how?

HANS

By employing your personality—and having success with yourself too. Suddenly I saw that I lacked something. And when I thought about it I realized that I lacked everything. For the first time I didn't just sort of exist for myself, but existed as someone who is comparable, say, with you. I couldn't bear the comparing any more, began to dream, evaluated myself. Incidentally, you just interrupted me and it was important. (*He sits down and closes his eyes. He shakes his head.*) Too bad. It's over. I felt really connected when I was dreaming. (*To* QUITT) I don't want to have to go on shaking my head much longer.

QUITT

It occurs to me I should have gotten you up earlier. Then you wouldn't get ideas like this. So you want to leave me?

HANS

On the contrary, I want to stay forever. I still have much to learn from you.

QUITT

Would you like to be like me?

HANS

I have to be. Recently I've been forcing myself to copy your handwriting. I no longer write with a slant but vertically. That is like standing up after a lifetime of bowing down. But it hurts, too. I also no longer put my hands like this . . . (*Thumbs forward, fingers backward on his hips*) on my hips, but like you do . . . (*Fingers forward, thumbs backward*) That gives me more self-confidence. Or standing up . . . (*He stands up.*) I stand on one leg and play with the other like you. A new sense of leisure. Only when I buy something, say at the butcher's, I place my legs quite close together and parallel and don't move from the spot. That makes an upper-class impression, and I always get the best cut and the freshest calf's liver. (*He yawns.*) Have you noticed that I no longer yawn as unceremoniously as I used to, but with a pursed mouth, like you?

QUITT
The long and short of it: you are still here for me?

HANS
Because I am compelled to be as free as you are. You have everything, live only for yourself, don't have to make any comparisons any more. Your life is poetic, Mr. Quitt, and poetry, as we know, produces a sense of power that oppresses no one—but rather dances the dance of freedom for us, the oppressed. At one time I felt caught in the act even when someone watched me licking stamps. Now I don't bat an eyelash when someone calls me a lackey; carry the garbage can out onto the sidewalk in my tails absolutely unfazed; walk self-confidently arm in arm with the ugliest woman; do work, willy-nilly, which isn't mine to do—that is my free-dom, which I have learned from you. In the past I used to be envious of what you could afford to do. I didn't feel treated like a man but like a mannequin—notice my new freedom, I'm already playing with words!—cursed you under my breath as a bloodsucker, did not see the human being in you, but only the corporation mogul. That's how unfree I was. Now, as soon as I imagine you, I see the self-assured curve that your watch chain describes over your belly and already I am moved.

QUITT
This sounds familiar. (HANS *laughs.*) So you're just making fun of me. I should have known that someone with your history would never change. But you're not the one who matters. It's the others that count.

HANS
Do you actually despise yourself, Mr. Quitt?— Now that you've screwed them all?

QUITT

Myself? No. But I might despise someone *like* me. (*Long pause.*) Why don't you react? Just now when you weren't answering me, what I said began to crawl back into me and wanted to make itself unsaid, and me too, by shriveling me deep inside. (*Pause.*) You're making fun of my language. I would much prefer to express myself inarticulately like the little people in the play recently, do you remember? Then you would finally pity me. This way I suffer my articulateness as part of my suffering. The only ones that you and your kind pity are those who can't speak about their suffering.

HANS

How do you want to be pitied? Even if you became speechless with suffering your money would speak for you, and the money is a fact and you—you're nothing but a consciousness.

QUITT

(*Derisively*) Pity only occurred to me because the characters in the play moved me so—not that they were speechless, but that despite their seemingly dehumanized demeanor they wanted really to be as kind to each other as we spectators who all live in more human surroundings are already with each other. They, too, wanted tenderness, a life together, et cetera—they just can't express it, and that is why they rape and murder each other. Those who live in inhuman conditions represent the last humans on stage. I like that paradox. I like to see human beings on the stage, not monsters. Human beings, gnarled with suffering, unschematic, drenched with pain and joy. The animalistic attracts me, the defenseless, the abused and insulted. Simple people, do you understand? Real people whom I can feel and taste, living people. Do you know what I mean? People! Simply . . . people! Do you know what I mean? Not fakes but . . .

(*He thinks for quite a while.*) people. You understand:
people. I hope you know what I mean.

HANS

I can't take your jokes so soon after waking up. But let's
suppose you're being serious. There must be another possibility which makes your dichotomy—here fakes, there
human beings—look ridiculous.

QUITT
Which?

HANS
I don't know.

QUITT
Why not?

HANS
That I don't know is the very thing that lends me hope.
Besides, as one of those whom you have in mind: I can say
it: every time when the curtain rises I become discouraged
at the prospect that things will be human again up there any
moment now. Let's further assume that you mean what you
say: perhaps the people on stage moved you—not because
they were people, but because everything was shown as it is.
For example, if you recognize a portrait as true to life, you
frequently develop a peculiar sympathy for the person in the
portrait without necessarily having any feeling for the real
person. Couldn't the same thing have happened to you when
you saw the play? That you empathized with the inarticulate
people represented there on the stage and think, therefore,
that you have done with the real ones? And why do you want
to see real characters on stage at all, who belong in the past
and are alien to you?

QUITT
Because I like to think back to the days when I was poor too, and couldn't express myself, and primarily because the painted grimaces from my own class sit in the audience anyway. On stage I want to see the other class, as crude and as unadorned as possible. After all, I go to the theater to relax.

HANS
(*Laughs.*) So, you *are* being derisive.

QUITT
I meant that seriously. (*He laughs. Both of them laugh.*)

(WIFE *enters.*)

HANS
Here comes one of your real people.

WIFE
Are you laughing at me?

QUITT
Who else?

WIFE
And what were you saying about me?

HANS
Nothing. We were only laughing about you.

(WIFE *laughs too; she slaps* QUITT *on the shoulder, nudges him in the ribs.*)

QUITT
We're all merry for once, right?

HANS
Since business is so good, Mr. Quitt—why don't you cross my palm with silver?

QUITT
You're welcome.

(*He wants to put the coin into* HANS's *outstretched hand but* HANS *pulls back the hand and stretches out the other. Now* QUITT *wants to put the coin into that hand, but* HANS, *so as to adjust to* QUITT, *has already stretched out his first hand again. When he notices that* QUITT . . . *he stretches out his second hand again. But* QUITT *tries to put the coin into* HANS's *first hand again and in the meantime, etc. Until* QUITT *puts the coin away again, walks to the piano, and plays a boogie.* WIFE *takes* HANS *and dances with him . . . Then* QUITT *suddenly plays a slow, sad blues and sings along with it.*)

QUITT
Sometimes I wake up at night
and everything I want to do next day
suddenly seems silly,
how silly to button your shirt,
how silly to look in your eyes,
how silly the foam on the glass of beer,
how silly to be loved by you.

Sometimes I lie awake
and everything I imagine
makes everything that much more inconceivable—
inconceivable the pleasure of standing at a hot-dog stand,
inconceivable New Zealand,
inconceivable thinking of sooner or later,
inconceivable to be alive or dead

I want to hate you and hate plastic,
you want to hate me and hate the fog.
I want to love you and love hilly countrysides,
you would like to love me
and have a lovely city, a lovely color, a lovely animal.

Everyone stay away from me,
it is the time after my death
and what I just imagined, with a sigh, as my life
are only blisters on my body
which sigh when they burst

(*He stops singing.*) But things are going well for us right now, aren't they? I saw a woman walking in the sun with a full shopping bag and I knew at once: Nothing more can happen to me now! I hear an old lady say: "Parsley on the stalk? I've never eaten that." And then she says: "Well, and I don't think I'll indulge in it now." Nothing can happen to me any more! Nothing can happen to me any more! (*He continues to sing.*)

No dream
could make anything seem stranger
than what I've already experienced
and there's no cure
for the peace and quiet

(*He speaks again.*) . . . with which every morning I let the dingaling out from behind my fly to fidget in the peep show to relieve the pressure which I could no longer imagine during the sleepless night. (VON WULLNOW, KOERBER-KENT, *and* LUTZ *appear silently.* WIFE *wants to leave.*) Stay here. (*She leaves.* HANS *leaves too. Pause.*) So you still exist. (*Pause.*) Why don't we make ourselves comfortable? (*Pause.*) What can I offer you? Schnapps? Cognac?

KOERBER-KENT
No, thank you. It's still too early for that.

QUITT
Or juice, freshly squeezed.

KOERBER-KENT
That doesn't agree with my stomach. Hyperacidity.

QUITT
Then a few breadsticks. Or would you prefer some other snack?

LUTZ
Thank you, we really don't want anything. Seriously, don't go to any trouble.

QUITT
You've got a frog in your throat. Hans will make you a camomile tea. (LUTZ *shakes his head.*) Camomile which we picked ourselves at the Mediterranean. The blossoms are intact!

LUTZ
(*Clears his throat.*) I'm over it already. I don't need anything.

QUITT
And you, Monsignore? Perhaps you'd like a mint lozenge? One hundred percent pure peppermint.

KOERBER-KENT
I'm perfectly happy too.

QUITT
I'd put it on your tongue myself.

KOERBER-KENT
I usually enjoy sucking on mint lozenges, but not today.

QUITT
Why not today? It isn't Friday, is it?

KOERBER-KENT
I simply don't want to. That's all.

QUITT
You want to jilt me?

KOERBER-KENT
If that's how you take it.

QUITT
I'm offended.

(*He walks out.* KOERBER-KENT *wants to make a gesture to stop him but* VON WULLNOW *makes a sign not to.*)

VON WULLNOW
I know. I could cut off his head with one slash of the whip and let the decapitated chicken slap on the table before you. I was grinding my teeth so fiercely just now, some must have cracked. (*He shows his teeth.*) There! You traitor, you upstart, you Polack! (*Raving*) My hand even trembled briefly, which almost never happens to me. In the meantime, of course, it has become completely steady again. Look! (*He holds out his hand.*) But we have to be rational now, in the most economic sense of the word: at first as rational as necessary and then, when he no longer has any need for our reason, as irrational as possible. I'm already looking forward to my irrationality. (*He makes a pantomime of trampling, torturing, and throttling.*)

LUTZ

(*Interrupts him.*) Yes, that's it; we have to let ourselves go for a moment. Like you just now. Perhaps that'll teach us what to do next. Let's say or do whatever comes to mind. That will determine our method. After all, that's the way he does it. So let's dream. (*Pause. They concentrate. Pause.*) Nothing is happening. I only see myself cutting a steak against the grain or playing tennis in such short pants that my testicles are hanging out on one side. (*Pause. They concentrate.*) Do you know what I'm most afraid of about myself? (*They regard him expectantly.*) That one day I will get up in a restaurant so lost in thought that I forget to pay the check.

(*Pause.* KOERBER-KENT *scratches his behind and they regard him.*)

KOERBER-KENT

I just happened to think of our minority stockholder . . .

(*Pause.*)

LUTZ

Don't you ever dream?

KOERBER-KENT

Ah! Monstrous dreams!

LUTZ

Well! Let's hear.

KOERBER-KENT

(*Powerfully*) I . . . I'm walking in the woods alone . . .

(*Long, embarrassed silence. Pause.* VON WULLNOW *laughs.*)

LUTZ
You are laughing?

VON WULLNOW
I was remembering.

LUTZ
Was it that funny?

VON WULLNOW
Remembering it was. (*Pause.*) The grain bins in the loft, the trickling grain and the mouse shit inside, the swirl of grain that my memory delved into like a boy's naked foot, the grains between the toes, the vacated wasp nest, still so enlivened by memories, on the underside of the roof tile. (*Pause.*) I've got to stop. Remembering makes me a good person. Otherwise I would make up in a moment. Oh, Quitt. Oh, Quitt, why hast thou forsaken us?

LUTZ
Now I know what we are going to do. We have to talk about ourselves, about us as individuals—what we're really like. I for one sometimes feel like hopping up and down on the street and don't do it. Why not? And last summer passed by without my having enjoyed it once while I was sitting in my office with its tinted window. Every so often I do something crazy: I eat the rotten part of an apple, slam a car door before everyone's gotten out . . . or something like that . . . and if that doesn't help, there's always . . . (*To* KOERBER-KENT) our minority stockholder. (QUITT *returns.*) He'll show him where the moon is rising.

QUITT
I do miss you. And perhaps you miss me too.

VON WULLNOW

Quitt, today I had a bag of flour in my hand. Do you know how long it has been since I've held flour in my hands? I don't even know myself. The package was so soft and heavy. This weight in my hand and at the same time the gentleness of the pressure—I was transported into delicious unreality. Doesn't the same thing ever happen to you?

QUITT

I find the most vicious reality more bearable than the most delicious feeling of unreality.

LUTZ

(*Trying to distract*) How is your wife?

QUITT

My wife? My wife is fine.

LUTZ

She looked well just now. With her cheeks all rosy as though she'd just played tennis. That made me think of my wife, who has to rock the child all day long on the terrace. You know, we have a retarded child who screams as soon as we stop rocking: my wife stands days on end in the garden and pushes the swing, imagine that. But she's gotten to like doing it nowadays. She says that it calms her down too. And she feels it makes her superior to the other women in the neighborhood who can't think of anything to do but tell their cleaning women how to do chores. By the way, excuse me for talking about myself.

QUITT

I like women who do nothing but give orders.

VON WULLNOW

I know you like hearing stories, I have one.

QUITT
Is it long?

VON WULLNOW
Very brief. A child walks into a shop and says, "Six rolls, the *Daily News*, and three salt sticks!"

QUITT
Go on.

VON WULLNOW
That's the story.

(*Pause.*)

QUITT
It's beautiful.

VON WULLNOW
(*Suddenly embraces him vehemently.*) I knew you would like it. I knew it. I'm usually too shy to touch anyone, but this time I simply must. (*He pulls* QUITT'*s cuffs out of his jacket, takes his hand.*) I've been looking at this dirty finger-nail all the time—now I have to clean it for you. (*He does so, using his own fingernail, steps back.*) I don't know what's the matter with me. I'm blissed out with memories recently. Do you remember that time we dressed up as workers at the opera ball? With red bandanas, T-shirts, high-pegged pants, and muddy boots. The way we stepped on the ladies' toes? The way we scratched our crotches? Staring at everything, our mouths agape? Ordered Crimean champagne and drank out of the bottle? And at the end pushed our caps back and sang the "Internationale"?

QUITT
Crimean champagne is an illegal label. It should be called "Sparkling Wine from the Crimea." (*Pause.*) Yes, we

played the part very expertly, so that we could only play ourselves.

VON WULLNOW
And now you're in cahoots with them.

QUITT
How so?

VON WULLNOW
By thinking only of yourself. The huge share of the market which you control provides the enemies of the free-enterprise system, who are our enemies too, with the welcome opportunity—

LUTZ
(*Interrupts him. Quickly*) Not like that. (*To* QUITT) I've been thinking a lot about death lately. Everything I encounter looks like a sign to me. When I read in the papers "Next Wednesday, junk collection," then I sense at once: "That junk, that's me." Recently when I entered a tobacco shop somewhere out in the country I saw an obituary pinned up on the wall—and under the obituary lay a filthy, shriveled-up glove: that leather glove, that'll soon be me, my heart fluttered.

QUITT
And I recently saw an empty plastic bag in a hallway with the legend "Hams from Poland" on it. Should that have been a sign too? In any event, I suddenly felt incredibly safe when I read that.

LUTZ
Don't you ever think of death?

QUITT
I can't.

VON WULLNOW
(*Strikes his fist against his forehead.*) And I can't any more!
I'd like to open a newspaper now and read the word *asshole*
in it. This jungle. This slime. This swamp. These will-o'-the-
wisps. (LUTZ *has nudged him with his elbow and* VON WULL-
NOW *calms down.*) These will-o'-the-wisps above the swamp
when we used to walk home in fall after our dancing lessons!
Wanda on my arm, I could feel her goose bumps through
her blouse, and a pheasant screamed in its sleep as I kissed
her—an ugly word actually, kissing—only the cracks of our
lips touch each other, as unfeeling as peeled-off bark. (*Pause.*
VON WULLNOW *looks at* LUTZ, *who gives him the cue by
forming the word* nature *with his lips.*) Why nature? Of
course, I was about to talk about nature: it was nature that
made me aware—by teaching me how to perceive. Houses,
streets, and I were just a daydream at first, dreamer and
what he dreamed were in the same bubble where the
dreamer—hypnotized by the invariably same, never-changing
spot on the buckling house wall, grown together in his sleep
with the same street curve day in and day out—also con-
sidered himself part of his dream. Dark spots inside me as
the only thing undefined. Then the bubble burst and the
dark spots *inside* me unfolded like the forests *outside* me.
Only then did I begin to define myself as well. Not the
civilization of house and street, but *nature* made me aware of
myself—by making me aware of nature. So: only in the per-
ception of nature, not in the hallucinatory hodgepodge of
the objects of civilization, can we arrive at our own history.
But nowadays most people have become so civilized that
they simply dismiss rapport with nature as some kind of
withdrawal into childhood—although it is children whom
one keeps having to make artificially aware of nature—or,

even if they pretend to have rapport with nature, cannot endure this nature without the mirage of civilization: inside the forest they have no feeling for the forest; except from the perspective of the window of their terraced house which they designed and built themselves, and which they would immediately sell to someone—only then would the same forest be an experience of nature for them. You're going to ask me what I mean by all this.

QUITT
No.

VON WULLNOW
I mean to say that you, you with your ruthless overexpansion, are destroying our nature. You senselessly transform the old countryside where we could come to our senses into construction sites. Your blind department stores squat like live bombs in our old city centers. Every day a new branch goes up, differing from the others only by its tax identification number, which you even set up in neon light to blink from its roof as an advertisement of your sense of public responsibility!

QUITT
A good idea, isn't it?

VON WULLNOW
You're ruining our reputation by carrying on just the way the Joneses think a businessman behaves.

QUITT
Perhaps it's not our reputation I'm ruining but you.

VON WULLNOW
You know neither honor nor shame. The manure pit behind my country house is too good for you. I'd like to choke you

by stuffing blotting paper down your throat. I damn you! Whosoever utters your name before me, there shall I reach into his mouth and rip out his tongue, and with my very own hands in fact. Wait, I'm going to step on your foot. (*He does so, not that* QUITT *reacts.* VON WULLNOW *blows up his cheeks and slaps them with his hands. He bites the back of his hand. He hits his head with his fist, quickly touches up his hair.*) You've disappointed me, Quitt. It's a pity about you. I liked you best of all. We've got so much in common. I still admire you. Whenever I have to reach a decision I think of what you would do under the same circumstances. (*He screams*) You rat, you Judas, for twenty pieces of silver—

QUITT
Thirty, to be exact.

VON WULLNOW
Twenty, I say.

QUITT
(*To* KOERBER-KENT) But thirty is right, isn't it?

KOERBER-KENT
Yes, it was thirty pieces of silver. According to the latest findings, it's a question of—

VON WULLNOW
(*Screaming*) Pervert! Atavist! (LUTZ *places a hand on his shoulder.*) I once dreamed that we grew old together. Every day we drove in a carriage through town, playing bridge. And now all that is supposed to remain a dream? Let's stop fighting each other, Quitt. It could be so beautiful—just the four of us—that is, five, counting Mrs. Tax—and since all the others have thrown in the towel in the meantime, we lone wolves have become so big there's no longer any need for arrangements. Those who help us into our coats after

our conferences could conduct our affairs for us. Let's not underbid each other any more.

QUITT
I underbid *you.* (VON WULLNOW *roars.*) Does it help?

VON WULLNOW
A hobnailed boot in your privates! Don't you understand me! What am I at this moment? A radical! How I'd simply like to yawn at you. Do you have a slice of bread on you?

QUITT
Are you hungry?

VON WULLNOW
I'd like to have something to crumble between my fingers. My brain is scraping against my brain pan. Actually a pleasant sensation. So animalistic. (*To* LUTZ) I won't say anything more now. (*To* QUITT) I'd like to switch with you, you shark. Besides, it's time for your wife to pass through the room again, isn't it? Come on, say something, I'd like to have something to laugh about! Dear Hermann . . . (*Pause. He takes* QUITT's *arm.*) You know, I could be your father? Let's go fishing together, fathers always take their sons fishing. Up the stream before the thunderstorm hits. I'd like to be drunk now so that I could remember something. (*He lets go of* QUITT's *arm.*) Apropos streams. You ruin them with your plastic monsters, let the countryside choke on plastic still lives stamped "biodegradable" where no environment is even left or, at most, a multicolored mildew on the ground, a soot-colored dust on a sweetly crinkling leaf, a fish belly in the churning water. Do you know what children ask when they're actually shown a big ripe tomato? Is it made of plastic? they ask. And I personally saw a child that didn't want to sit down in a Rolls-Royce because the seat wasn't made of plastic. Let's stop all this overexpansion,

Hermann—or let's limit ourselves to products for environmental protection. There's still a pretty penny to be made in that field. Everything could be the way it used to be.

QUITT

But you stopped expanding a long time ago. Besides, as you say so rightly, the functional units are diminishing in size. So the number of units can continue to increase, right? I'm not the kind of man who wants to leave everything the way it is. I can't see anything without wanting to utilize it. I want to make everything I see into something else. And so do you! Except that you can't any more.

VON WULLNOW

(*Steps away from* QUITT.) You refuse to understand us.

QUITT

I understand you very well. You know what it means when one of us becomes human or even speaks about death. An emotion, after the first moment of fright, becomes a method for us.

VON WULLNOW

It's not that I call your behavior treason—but what should I call it? Faithlessness? Treachery? Unreliability? Falseness? Cuntiness? Disloyalty?

QUITT

Those are the expressions you apply to employees. Among us I would call it businesslike behavior.

VON WULLNOW

Now I really won't say anything more. I'll stick my finger down my throat in front of you. (*Does so and leaves, but returns at once.*) And I really was attached to you. (*He leaves and returns.*) You with your frog's body. (*He leaves and returns.*) My spit is too good for you. All I'll do is spit it from the back to the front of my mouth. (*Does so, leaves once more, returns once more, is beside himself, makes a horrible face, and leaves once and for all.*)

(LUTZ *wants to say something.*)

QUITT
I know what you want to say.

LUTZ
Then you say it.

QUITT
It's true. I didn't stick to our agreement.

LUTZ
But you didn't plan it that way.

QUITT
I simply forgot about it, did I?

LUTZ
Not exactly forgot perhaps, but you didn't take it seriously enough.

QUITT
Why should I have taken it seriously?

LUTZ
(*Laughs.*) Not bad. Very tricky indeed . . . (*Pause.*) Excuse me, I interrupted you. You were going to say something.

QUITT
No, that was it.

LUTZ
Why don't you defend yourself?

QUITT
Why don't you accuse me?

LUTZ
You must be very unhappy.

QUITT
Why?

LUTZ
One is completely locked up inside oneself like you only when one is miserable. I know that from my own experience.

QUITT
Don't compare me with yourself.

LUTZ
There, you see. For you there's only you, you don't even want to be compared. You must be in pretty bad shape. (*He's been playing with his forefinger and thumb the whole time, unconsciously, as though he were counting money.*)

   (QUITT *takes hold of his hand.*)

QUITT
Why don't you admit it: that's nothing but your new gesture for something tangible? Anyway, you've been counting money ever since you started to talk.

LUTZ
All right. Now I'm going to tell you what I think of you.

QUITT
But watch out. Perhaps you'll think differently once you've begun to speak.

LUTZ

Once I begin to speak everything is completely thought out. I don't stutter. (*To* KOERBER-KENT) He multiplied his share of the market at our expense. I have nothing against his methods, but he should have discussed them with us. And besides, of course I do have something against his methods: he recruits the ex-convicts away from us in the labor market and promises them a sympathetic environment—and that means that he leaves them entirely to themselves in a certain area of production and pays all of them the same low wages. As he admitted just now, he manufactures smaller and smaller amounts of his products but without changing the size of the package, so that the buyers believe they're getting the same amount. This way his prices appear to remain the same while we have to raise ours. He lets doctors buy shares in his drug firms and then they prescribe his medicines. (*To* QUITT) You duplicate our most expensive products with cheap materials. Your guarantees are only valid for Three-Star refrigerators. You print the national eagle on your retail price tags, so that it looks as though they are government-approved. Your price tags are huge—so that people believe your things are cheaper even when they are at least as expensive as anywhere else. The price structure has cracked, Quitt. We are standing at the deathbed—at the deathbed of the old concept of price—and have gotten sore feet ourselves. We shiver in the shadow of your competition. As far as I'm concerned, I'm still far too calm. Perhaps that is the calm before the next breach of the agreement, which will be my downfall. I can already see the hailstorm in the distance, and panic flattens my ears against my head. I'm afraid, Quitt, afraid of the great storm when I won't be wearing the thick coat of capital. And yet I tried to save the structure by firing thousands. Quitt, you ruined our prices. You pushed them down to prewar levels! Everything has a slight crack. Every day there's one product less on the market. It's

all over with the beautiful diversity of the market. Even the
high consecration is for nothing. It's the end of all our
proud figures. I'm at a loss. I am at a most poodle-befuddled
loss and in utter despair. (*To* KOERBER-KENT) I was my
parents' only child. Even my birth was a practical decision:
it meant my mother's death. At age four I kneaded imita-
tion coins out of mud. At age seven I picked flowers for
invalids in the neighborhood and sold them. In school they
called me "Moneybags." A sensible boy, my father said. He
still has respect for material values, said my relatives. Before
my first communion, the priest said that if you really wanted
something afterward and really believed it, the wish would
come true. Still feeling the pressure of the host against my
gums, I walked all the way home with my head lowered:
because every cell of my body believed I would find the coin
I had wished for. (*To no one in particular*) Since that time
I've had my doubts about religion. (*To* KOERBER-KENT) But
I remained reasonable and became more and more reasonable. He's all business, people said of me. But now it's all
over. All over. I don't want to believe anything any more.
What's there left to believe in if that s.o.b. destroys our
prices and our rational system? What kind of age is that?
What's still valid? I too want to be unbusinesslike at last!
(*Pause.*) I dreamed that I was running and kept on running
so that a huge banknote wouldn't fall off my chest. Just
the way I keep on talking now. I'd like to put my head into
a bowl of water and drown myself. (*Exit.*)

(KOERBER-KENT *wants to follow him but returns again.*
QUITT *paces up and down.*)

KOERBER-KENT
(*With lowered head*) I don't envy you, Quitt. I could also
tell you about myself, like the others, but that's not my way.
I never talk about myself. I'm proud that I eliminated myself
from my own calculations long ago. I'm not interested in

poking around the lint in my navel. I'm glad that I can be replaced. (*Pause.*) I pity you, Quitt. And I'm afraid for you. I recently saw a drawing a painter made of his dying wife: the pupils had lost almost all their color in the fever, and the iris, too, had become very pale. Nothing but a dark circle separated it from the white of the eye around it, and the centrifugal force of dying had even thickened this circle. It was as if the eyes sighed toward the observer. The artist's pencil had hatched an endless sea of sighs from a mortal seeing hole, as I called it. And the following morning the woman is supposed to have really died. (*A popping sound backstage.*) What was that?

QUITT
Hans is at work. He isn't very good at uncorking bottles. There's almost always a pop when he opens the cooking wine.

(*Pause.*)

KOERBER-KENT
Aren't you afraid to die? (*He raises his head and wants to transfix* QUITT—*but* QUITT *happens to be standing behind him.*)

QUITT
Over here.

KOERBER-KENT
Don't you ever quickly push everything away from you just because you are deathly afraid? (QUITT *steps away from him and comes to a halt with his back to him.* KOERBER-KENT *lowers his head again and closes his eyes.*) Someone once told me how he dreamed he was dying. He was sitting on a sled and said: I am dying. Then he was dead, and at some point they closed the coffin lid over him. And only then did

he become deathly afraid: he didn't want to be buried. He woke up, his heart was fibrillating. Besides, he was very ill, the dream wanted to kill him. Cause of death: a dream, you could say. (*Very loudly*) You see, dying in your sleep isn't at all peaceful, but perhaps the worst death of all.

(QUITT *has kept pacing around in the meantime, absentmindedly, and now stands in front of* KOERBER-KENT.)

QUITT
(*Very softly*) Really?

KOERBER-KENT
(*Is startled. Looks up at* QUITT *now.*) I know from other stories (*One can hear a key turning in a lock backstage and a door handle being pressed down.*) that a dying person keeps looking away whenever his eye catches a specific object, as though he could postpone death in this way . . . (*He listens.*) Someone pushed down a door handle just now, no? Why don't I hear a door opening? (*Pause.*) Once during a meal I personally sat opposite a man who suddenly started putting the table in order: put the knife and fork parallel to each other, wiped the edge of the glass with his napkin, shoved the napkin into its silver ring. Then he keeled over dead.

QUITT
(*Distracted*) Who kneeled on the bread?

KOERBER-KENT
He keeled over dead, I said. (*Frightened*) You're afraid too.

QUITT
(*Scratching his pants absentmindedly*) Damnit, the cleaner didn't get that spot out either. Yes? I'm listening.

KOERBER-KENT

He was still smiling beforehand—(*Two or three distinctly audible steps backstage.*) but in his deathly fear he bared his *lower* teeth instead of his upper teeth, as you would expect. Nothing wrong with a dead dwarf, that's still a vegetative process, almost. But a *fully grown* corpse, just imagine that! It's monstrous. (*He listens.*) Why doesn't he walk on? Wasn't someone just walking back there?

QUITT

My baby fat starts growing back when I listen to you. You and your deathly fear—at the moment everything seems thinkable to me and also beside the point.

KOERBER-KENT
What? What?

QUITT
It was just the floor creaking, I'm sure of it.

   (PAULA *appears in a dress and with a veil in front of her face. At the sight of her,* QUITT *unzips his fly halfway down and up again. A garbage can cover bangs loudly on a hard floor backstage.*)

KOERBER-KENT

As I said, I've got an eye for those who are marked. (*He points to* QUITT.) It's that thin line on the upper lip . . . (*He notices* PAULA.) It's you! How good that you are here. Perhaps you could . . . him . . . (*He tries to find the word.*) What's the word?

QUITT
Congratulate him?

KOERBER-KENT
No.

QUITT
Work on him?

KOERBER-KENT
Something like that . . . no.

QUITT
Take him over your knees?

KOERBER-KENT
(*Panic-stricken*) Oh, God, how did this happen? I can't find the right word any more. What are they doing to me? Come down, eclipse of the sun! Hellfire, burst forth from the earth!

(QUITT *walks up to* PAULA *and whispers in her ear.*)

PAULA
(*Loudly*) "Deathly afraid?" (*To* KOERBER-KENT) You are trying to make him deathly afraid? Do you think he'll admit us back into the market?

KOERBER-KENT
(*Screams*) I know what I'm talking about. I've seen thousands die in the war. (QUITT *sighs.* KOERBER-KENT *resumes normal tone of voice at once.*) Am I keeping you from something?

QUITT
Not at all.

KOERBER-KENT
(*Screams*) I can read signs. I know why you hunch up your shoulders when you walk around. But soon you will shoulder the necessary weight of death, no matter what, Hermann Quitt. Even if you dangle your arms back and forth like that and scurry every which way. Even if you sit up straight as a

candle in your deathly fear! (*He begins walking out back-ward.* HANS *appears, wearing his chef's hat.*) You won't even be able to imagine the moment. There will be nothing but abrupt, animalistic, anxiety-ridden anticipation. You will be so afraid you won't even dare to swallow, and the spit will turn sour in your mouth. Your death will be gruesome beyond all imaginings, complete with moaning and bellowing. I know what I'm talking about. With moaning and bellowing. (*He walks backward into* HANS *and emits a scream. Exit.*)

(HANS *also exits.* QUITT *and* PAULA *look at one another for a long time.*)

QUITT
If you keep looking at me, I will lose the rest of my feelings.

PAULA
I won.

QUITT
Why?

PAULA
Because you were the first to talk.

QUITT
Now it's your turn.

PAULA
I love you, still. (*She laughs.*)

QUITT
Why are you laughing?

PAULA
Because I succeeded in saying that.

QUITT

I can't buy myself anything with that.

PAULA

You are so artificial. You're sacrificing the truth now for a slick cliché.

QUITT

Moreover, I didn't give you any excuse for it. (*Pause.*) I keep having to get used to you all over again. (*He looks her over from head to foot.*)

PAULA

I'm not one of those.

QUITT

Who, after all, is one of those? (*Pause.*) I'm tired. When I take a step I feel as if my real body has stayed behind. I don't need you. When I saw you I was happy, but I also was a bit turned off. I took that as a sign that all my desire for you is gone.

(*She laughs. He regards her considerately until she has finished.*)

PAULA

What you say is supposed to humiliate me. But the voice that I hear flatters me.

QUITT

You've changed. You're out of breath. Before, when you used to show your feelings you used to be much more self-assured. Why can't it be that way now? Stop playing the humble woman. I only want to touch you when you talk matter-of-factly. (*Spitefully*) Incidentally, why are you by yourself and not with the team? Do you call that creative?

My head hurts. Besides, I like you better when you wear pants.

PAULA
Your head is also hurting me, yes, your whole life . . . (QUITT *pats her arm.*) You pat me the way a conductor raps his baton . . . (*She caresses him.*)

QUITT
Your caresses tickle me.

PAULA
Yes, because you don't want to enjoy them. (QUITT'S WIFE *enters. She is wearing the same dress as* PAULA. *She notices, stops, and leaves again.*) Now caress me too. (QUITT *caresses her and steps away from her.*) That was one too few. (QUITT *returns and caresses her once more.*) Oh yes. (*Pause.*) Tell me about yourself.

QUITT
(*Animatedly*) I was thirsty a few days ago. (*Pause.*) It just occurred to me.

PAULA
Look at me, please.

QUITT
I don't like to look at you.

PAULA
Well, what am I like?

QUITT
Unchanged.

PAULA

Before I got to know you better I thought you were unfeeling and tough. I once heard you say of me—the brunette there—as about a whore.

QUITT

You always tell yourself stories like that afterward.

PAULA

What would you say I would say now? Mr. Quitt?

QUITT

Don't call me that. (*She puts her hand on his shoulder. Suddenly she begins to choke him. He lets her do so for some time, then shakes her off.* QUITT's WIFE *has returned in a different dress. She watches, giggling inaudibly, sucking her thumb.* QUITT *seats himself in the deck chair and lowers his head.* PAULA *squats down and wants to take his head in her hands. He gives her a kick. She falls down and gets up, warbling. He kicks her again. She gets up, warbling. He wants to kick her again, but she eludes him, warbling.*) Your slimy tongue. Your absurd hips.

PAULA

(*Lifts her dress.*) Look at the way my thigh is twitching. Can you see it? Why don't you come closer? (QUITT *grunts.*) Come on.

(QUITT *puts his hand on her thigh.* PAULA *presses her head close to him. Pause.*)

QUITT

All right, get lost now. (*He steps back. Pause.*) The saliva in your mouth will run over in a moment. And the way your eyeballs jerk back and forth! (*He turns away. Pause.*)

PAULA
I'm going already. It's no use. I'll sell.

QUITT
(*Regards her.*) And I'll determine the fine print.

PAULA
Only promise me that you won't clean up the moment after I've left.

QUITT
Buying yourself a hat can be very comforting.

PAULA
Now I know why I like you. It's so easy to think of something else when you're talking.

QUITT
Tomorrow at this time it will already be lighter, or darker. Perhaps that will comfort you too.

PAULA
(*Suddenly embraces* QUITT's WIFE, *releases her, and tosses* QUITT *a friendly as well as a serious kiss as she walks out.*) "No hard feelings . . ."

(QUITT *throws a stool after her.* PAULA *exits.*
QUITT's WIFE *comes closer. They stand opposite each other, not saying anything. The stage light changes after some time. First sunshine, then cloud shadows moving across the two of them. Crickets chirp. Far off in the distance a dog barks. The sound of the ocean. A child screams something into the wind. Distant church bells. Woolly tree blossoms blow across the stage. Both of them as silhouettes in the dusk against the backdrop of city lights, which are just coming on. The noise of an airplane engine, very close, slowly*

receding—while previous stage lighting comes back on. Quiet.)

WIFE
(*Softly*) You look so unapproachable.

QUITT
Remembering does that. I'm just remembering. Let me be. I've got to remember to the end. (*He sits down on the deck chair. She steps closer. He touches her lightly with his foot.*)

WIFE
Yes?

QUITT
Nothing, nothing. (*He leans back and closes his eyes.*)

WIFE
(*Sighs.*) Oh.

QUITT
(*To himself*) So that it crashes and splinters . . .

WIFE
What will you do?

QUITT
(*To himself*) Stop. Destroy. (*He looks back at her.*) Strange: when I look at you, my thoughts skip a beat.

WIFE
I'd like to speak about myself for once too.

QUITT
Not again!

WIFE
Why, are you listening to me?

QUITT
You could have been talking about yourself while you asked that. Did you wash your hair?

WIFE
Yes, but not for you. I am not well.

QUITT
Then scream for help.

WIFE
When I scream for help, you reply by telling me a story how you once needed help. (*Pause. She laughs a few times in quick succession as though about something funny.* QUITT *doesn't react.*) Help!

QUITT
You have to shout at least twice.

WIFE
I can't any more.

QUITT
(*Gets up.*) Then do away with yourself. (*He turns away.*)

WIFE
(*Mechanically wipes the dandruff off his shoulders.*) You're up to something. I can't look at you for too long, otherwise I'll find out what.

QUITT
What do you want? I have a pink face, my body is warm, pulse eighty.

(*Pause.*)

WIFE
My eyes are burning. I'm so sad I forgot to blink.

QUITT
What's there to eat today?

WIFE
Filet of veal with truffles.

QUITT
I see. Well, well. Interesting. W*hat* is there to eat today?

WIFE
But you just asked that. Why are you so distracted?

QUITT
(*To himself*) Because every possibility has been tried except the very last one, and that one shouldn't turn into just another idle mental exercise! Of course, filet of veal with truffles, you said so—I hear it only now. Why am I so distracted? I have to tell you something, my dear.

(*A pause. She looks at him.*)

WIFE
No, please don't say it. (*She shies back.*)

QUITT
I have to tell someone.

WIFE
(*Shies back and holds her ears shut.*) I don't want to hear it.

QUITT
(*Follows her.*) You'll know it in a moment.

WIFE

Don't say it, please don't. (*She runs away and he follows her. Quiet. Pause. She returns, slowly, walking backward, and goes off again, not that one sees her face.*)

(KILB *storms in.* HANS *appears behind him, wearing the chef's hat.* KILB *is holding a knife and runs back and forth.*)

KILB

You have to die now. It's no use. I'm alone. No one pays me. Not even they. It's our last way out. Don't contradict me. (*He notices that there's no one present, and puts the knife back in his pocket.*) He isn't even here! And I rehearsed it so well! Into the room and right at him! One, two. A picture without words, only dashes for the caption underneath.

HANS

You have to try again.

KILB

I have to concentrate once more for that. If I'm as unconcentrated as I am now, everything could just as easily be something else, I think, even I myself. And that is a hideous feeling. Leave me alone.

HANS

But look at me first: because it's really me now. People used to say about me: That fellow, it's eating him up inside, but one day he'll blow his stack and the walls will come tumbling down. That moment has come. So I will leave the room and cook the truffled filet with special tenderness, thinking how it will be left over for me. I leave Mr. Quitt to his fate, he believes in things like that. First of all, I'm going to stick to myself and I am curious what that will bring. My big toe is already itching, a good sign; I'm becoming human.

KILB
How?

HANS
Because an itching big toe means that you should remember something, and someone who remembers becomes a human being. So all I need to do is remember.

There was a time something inside me wanted to scream
At the mere thought that I might dream.
Now I want to learn to dream without end
So that the floor of facts I might transcend.
My eyes I want to learn to close
So as to know more of the little I knows.
In my youth a palm reader told me a fable
That I would be able
To change the world's plan.
I hereby announce that at least *my* world is changing.
(*He quickly punches the balloon punching-bag fashion. The balloon bursts.* HANS *exits.*

 KILB *concentrates, puts the stool on its legs, gently closes the cover of the piano, puts in order what needs putting into order.*

 QUITT *returns.*)

KILB
Not yet!

QUITT
You again.

KILB
But we haven't seen each other in ages.

QUITT

Not ages enough. Recently I thought of a mistake I once made. I couldn't remember what kind of mistake it had been—but I was sure at once that it was not an important mistake. Later on I remembered more distinctly: it had been an important mistake after all. It occurred to me only when I was dealing with you.

KILB

Please stay like that.

(*Pause.*)

QUITT

Kilb, I'm happy that you came. And please note that I said "I'm happy" and not "it makes me happy."

KILB

Please don't become too friendly now. (*Pause.* QUITT *regards him for a long time.*) Why are you looking at me?

QUITT

I'm only too tired to look elsewhere. Why don't *you* at least sit down, so that I won't become even more tired. (*He points to the deck chair.*)

KILB

No, that's too deep for me, I'll never be able to get out of it. (QUITT *sits down in it.*) Particularly if you keep your hands in your pockets the way you do. *I* always keep my hands out of my pockets in moments of danger.

QUITT

Kilb, nothing is possible any longer. I feel like I'm the sole survivor, and I find it unappetizing that there's nothing left except me. If only there were an appetizing explanation for this state of affairs—but my awareness is the awareness of a pile of garbage in an infinite empty space. Imagine: the telephone no longer rings, the postman doesn't come any more, all street noises have ceased, only the wind is rustling one dream further away—the world has already died. I'm the only one who hasn't heard of the catastrophe. I'm actually only a phantom of myself. What I see are afterimages, what I think are afterthoughts. A hair bends over on my head and I'm frightened to death. The next moment will be the last and un-time will begin. Just a moment ago there was still a bubble where I was, but not any more. I know that my time is over. You were right, Paula.

KILB

Absolutely right. You're an anachronism, Mr. Quitt. Like the goose step of your soul right now.

QUITT

Be quiet. No one but I can say that. (*He bounces a little ball and looks at* KILB.) Now that it's just the two of us, instead of becoming different you only become afraid that you might become different. (*Pause.*) There is nothing unthought of any more. Even the Freudian slip from the unconscious has already become a management method. Even dreams are dreamed from the beginning so as to be interpretable. For example, I no longer dream anything that isn't articulated, and the pictures of the dream follow each other logically like the sequence of days in a diary. I wake up in the morning and am paralyzed with all the speeches I've heard in the dream. There's no longer the "and suddenly" of the old dreams. (*The ball escapes and rolls away.*) Oh, too bad . . . (*He gets up.* KILB *has approached.*) The chair really is too deep, you're right. When I think of myself, using precise concepts, I have one attack of nausea after the other. This businessman with a handkerchief in his breast pocket and his English worsted suit full of *Weltschmerz* on board his private

plane the soot from whose jets drifts down on the workers'
apartment projects, with organ music of the Old Masters
oozing from the built-in loudspeakers—stop it, get rid of it,
bomb it, it's logical. But: every logical conclusion is immediately contradicted within me by this totally indecisive
yet totally self-assured *feeling*.

KILB
It's logical. You want to go on living.

QUITT
The little man wants to put on airs.

KILB
Why not. What else has the little man left to put on?

QUITT
You're right. Why not? A good cue. I'm still stuck too deep
in my role. Spitefully I walk past the spastics in the V.A.
hospitals and look away when someone rummages in garbage
cans for food. Why do I do it, actually? There's scarcely
anyone who looks as if he could still fall out of his role. I once
walked on the street and suddenly noticed that I didn't have
anything to do with my face any more . . .

KILB
The old story with the masks.

QUITT
Yes, but now someone who experienced it is telling about it.
Outside, the muscles clung to the dead skin, then one dead
layer on top of the other, only inside, in the deepest center,
where I should have been, there was still a little twitching
and something wet. A car would have to crash into me at
once!— Only then would I stop making a face. And not
merely show my true face when I can't avoid the onrushing

car any more, I thought. But this dead skin, that already was
my true face.

KILB

Nothing but stories. Where's the connection?

QUITT

I don't know anything about myself ahead of time. My ex-
periences only occur to me in the telling. That establishes
the connection. I'm now going to tell you what is hell for
me: hell for me is the so-called bargain, what's cheap. In a
dark hour I happened into a restaurant which had the same
menu that people like me usually eat, only half as expensive—
but this wasn't the same food: the meat deep-frozen, thrown
into the pan and fried to death; the potatoes waterlogged; the
vegetables something slopped into the pot with the liquid
from the can; the paper napkin shredding after one wipe,
and tossed in as a freebie, a tablecloth with static elec-
tricity, which made the hairs on my fingers stand on end.
Pressed to the table because others sat next to and beside
me, the only view the frosted windowpane in front of which
the potted flowers flapped in the air from the heating vent.
Only a luxurious existence isn't a punishment, I thought.
Only the greatest luxury is worthy of a human being. What's
cheap is inhuman.

KILB

That's why your products are always the cheapest.

QUITT

How much do you want for your answer? For once, couldn't
I be the topic? Me—that's what makes me shy back, that's
what I have had enough of, up to here, and what still lies at
the tip of my tongue all the time—something as rare and
ridiculous as a living mole. I feel watched by all sides like the
dead flesh from a wound that has long since healed, and still

I dance on the inside with self-awareness. Yes, inside I'm dancing! I once sat in the sun in actual shock, the sun was shining on me, not that I felt it, and I really felt like the outline of suffocating nothingness in the airy space around me. But even that was still me, me, me. I was in despair, could think neither back nor forward—had no sense of history left. Each recollection came in dribs and drabs, unharmoniously, like the recollection of a sex act. This aching lack of feeling, that was myself, and I was not only I but also a quality of the world. Of course, I asked about the terms. Why? Why this condition? These conditions—why no history but only these conditions? But all the conditional requirements were fulfilled. No "whys" helped any more. Only the unconditional requirements remained. "I'm bored," a child once said. "Then play at something. Paint something. Read something. Do something," it was told. "But I can't, I'm bored," it said. (*He keeps taking objects from his pockets, looks at them, and puts them back again.*) The goose step of my soul, you said? I want to speak about (*Laughs.*) myself without using categories. I don't want to mean anything any more, please, not be a character in the story any more. I want to freeze at night in May. Look, these are photos of me: I look happy in all of them and yet I never was. Do you know the feeling when one has put a pair of pants on backward? One time I was happy: when I visited someone in a tenement and during a long pause in the conversation I could hear the toilet flushing in the apartment next door. I became musical with happiness! Oh, my envy of your sleepy afternoons in those tenements with their mysteriously gurgling toilet bowls! Those are the places I long for: the projects at the edge of the city where the telephone booths are lit up at night. To go into airport hotels and simply check oneself in for safekeeping. Why are there no depersonification institutes? How beautiful it used to be when you opened a new can of shoe polish! And I could still imagine buying a ham sandwich, looking at cemeteries, having something in common with someone. Sometimes one thing simply led exhilaratingly to the other—that's what it meant to feel alive! Now I'm heavy and sore and bulky with myself. (*He punches himself under his chin while talking, kicks his calf.*) One wrong breath and I disintegrate. Do you know that I hear voices? But not the kind of voices that madmen hear: no religious phrases, or poetry regurgitated from schooldays, or one-shot philosophies, none of the traditional formulas— but movie titles, pop tunes, advertising slogans. "Raindrops are falling on my head," it frequently resounds in a whisper in the echo chamber of my head, and in the middle of an embrace a voice interrupts me with "Guess who's coming to dinner?" or "I'd walk a mile for a Camel." And I am positive that in the future even madmen will hear only voices like that—no longer "Know thyself" or "Thou shalt honor thy father and mother . . ." the superego voices of our culture. While one set of monsters is being exorcised, the next ones are already burping outside the window. (*He interrupts himself.*) How odd: while I go on talking logically like this, I simultaneously see, for example, a wintry lake at dusk which is just beginning to freeze over, or a small tree with a bottle stuck on its top, and an unshaven Chinese who peers around a doorway—now he's gone again—and, moreover, during the whole time I keep humming a certain moronic melody inside myself. (*He hums.* KILB *wants to say something.*) No, I am speaking now. I am blowing my horn! The goose step of my soul. You should try it too. At least try . . . Stand still, why don't you! Do I spit when I talk? Yes, I can feel the spit bubbles on my teeth. But my time to speak isn't over yet. At one time I used to think, Let's hope the next world war doesn't start before my new suit is ready. By talking I want to have the transmission of consciousness, now, before you are finished with me. For too long my lips have held themselves joylessly shut. (*He suddenly embraces* KILB *and holds on to him.*) Why am I talking so fluently? Whereas I actually feel the need to stutter. (*He bends over*

and therefore presses KILB *more tightly.* KILB *is writhing.*)
I w . . . want to s . . . stutter . . . And why do I see
everything so distinctly? I don't want to see the grain in the
wood floor so distinctly. I'd like to be nearsighted. I'd like
to tremble. Why am I not trembling? Why am I not
stuttering? (*He bends over vehemently and* KILB *writhes.*) I
once wanted to sleep. But the room was so big. Wherever I
lay down I created spots of sleeplessness. The room was too
big for me alone. Where is the place to sleep here? Smaller!
Smaller! (*He bends over so much that* KILB *groans. He bends
even more and the groaning ceases.* KILB *falls on the floor
and doesn't move.* QUITT *crosses his arms. Pause.*) I can smell
the cologne he smelled of. (*Pause.*) How happy I became
once when I put on a shirt one of whose buttons had just
been sewn on. My shirt is torn. How beautiful! Then I wore
it long enough for it to become threadbare.

(*Pause.
A tremendous burping pervades the entire room.
Long pause.
The burping.
*QUITT *runs his head against the rock. After some time he
gets up and runs against the rock again. He gets up once
more and runs against the rock. Then he just lies there. The
stage light has been extinguished. Only the trough with the
risen dough, the melting block of ice, the shriveled balloon,
and the rock are lighted. A fruit crate trundles down, as
though down several steps, and comes to rest in front of the
rock. A long gray carpet rolls out from behind the rock:
snakes writhe on the rolled-out carpet and in the fruit crate.*)

**Translated by MICHAEL ROLOFF
in collaboration with Karl Weber**